By:

Clare Bevan.

Clare
Bevan.

Published by New Generation Publishing in 2021

Copyright © Clare Bevan 2021

First Edition

ISBN: 978-1-80031-129-9

www.newgeneration-publishing.com

New Generation Publishing

1.
INTRODUCTION.
****

(Christmas Tops And Tails !)

A LETTER TO YOU FROM CLARE BEVAN.

Hello and welcome to my 'Christmas Cracker'.

For more than thirty years, I have had fun organising a jolly
Christmas Show.

My merry Readers like to dress up in Christmassy clothes - and
they all have a great time making people smile.

My oldest ever Reader was Father Christmas, of course. And my
youngest was my little son. He was only ten months old - so he
was the Baby Jesus !

Now I hope YOU will enjoy these poems - and have a great time
dressing up too !

In this book, you will find: a naughty Donkey; a flock of Sheep;
a flying Pig; a grumpy Reindeer; some Christmas letters; a happy
Zoo-Keeper; a crowd of Pantomime Characters; a sad Penguin; a
spooky Fridge AND a Snowman's Smile !

So off you go - and please have FUN.

****

This book is for all the children in my family -
and especially for my two grandsons -
Elijah and Dylan.

CHRISTMAS CRACKERS.
****

Does it matter if the hats are simply hopeless ?
Does it matter that the gifts are cheap and small ?
Does it matter if the jokes are growing whiskers,
And the riddles almost drive us up the wall ?

But EVERYONE is having fun together -
And that's what really matters after all.

****

A BIG CHRISTMAS 'THANK YOU' PAGE.
****

First:

An enormous thank you to all my wonderful Readers.
The lovely Bracknell Drama Club Crew who have always read
my poems so splendidly - plus special thanks to Ann and Roger,
who turned my little Christmas collections into jolly-holly
booklets. All our brilliant Musicians, especially: Bea, John, Tim
and Kim. All the brave children who sang along and enjoyed the
fun ! And of course, dear old Ted who knew Father Christmas so
well.

****

Second:

All the friends and fans who have come along to our 'Poems
and Pies' shows. Some of you have been to EVERY show since
1985 ! And now our new audiences and readers in friendly
Crowthorne. You have helped us raise a great deal of money for
our local families, who are coping with Muscular Dystrophy -
thank you SO much.

****

Third:

Our 'Poems and Pies' friends from all over the country:
Axmouth; Canterbury; Ian Tracey and Readers from Liverpool
Cathedral; Stockport; The Wirral; Orkney; London; Croydon;
Stowupland, Henley and more.

****

Fourth

Famous Friends - especially Sir Richard Baker, who used my poems at the Barbican and on B.B.C. Radio Four - and gave me some merry ideas.

Dear Sir Ken Dodd and Lady Anne Dodd, who inspired so many of my favourite poems. Ken's festive voice is on our Answer Phone - so he can still give me a nudge when it's time to start a new set of cheery poems.

****

And finally, Martin and Ben - who have not only performed their poems brilliantly, but have also put out the chairs for the audience...and cleared up afterwards !
(More importantly, Martin is now our contact with good old Santa Claus !)

THANK YOU ALL.

****

(And if this book sells well, some of my profits will go to Muscular Dystrophy U.K.)

CONTENTS:

1. CHRISTMAS SINGERS.

****

****

2. CHRISTMAS AT SCHOOL.

****

3. CHRISTMAS AT HOME.

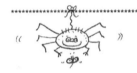

****

4. CHRISTMAS CREATURES.

****

****

5. CHRISTMAS CHARACTERS.

****

****

6. CHRISTMAS WITH SANTA.

****

****

7. CHRISTMAS AND AFTER.

****

****

CHRISTMAS SINGERS

THE SINGERS OF BETHLEHEM.

****

The father sang of journeys;
The donkey sang of sleep;
The shepherd sang of fearful dreams,
Of lamb's wool - warm and deep.

The pigeon sang of darkness;
The field-mouse sang of light;
The oxen sang of comfort
In the hollows of the night.

The tomcat sang of strangers;
The women sang of birth;
The angels sang of miracles,
Of joy for all the Earth.

The wise men sang of wonders
That gleamed amongst the straw -
But Mary sang of one dear child
To love
For ever more.

****

LISTEN.
****

Listen.
Far away, the swish of a donkey's tail,
The yawn of weary strangers,
The groan of a tired Inn Keeper
Who opens a creaky door -
Far away.

Listen.
Not so far, the rustle of straw,
The murmur of women offering kindness,
And the cry of a baby in its mother's arms -
Not so far.

Listen.
Closer now, the homely bleat of a sheep
Answering her lamb's quiet call.
The rattle of stones on a hillside path -
Closer now.

Listen.
Nearer still, the snort of a camel,
The whisper of silk as a king leans down
To place his gift in the rustling straw -
Nearer still.

Listen.
So close, you are almost there.
The singing of the stars,
The soundless flurry of wings,
The soft whimper of a sleepy child -
So close
You are almost there.

THE DONKEY'S CHRISTMAS TALE.
****

One winter, when journeys were harder than now,
A man asked his neighbour to help him - somehow.
"My friend," said the Farmer, "I'll lend you my donkey -
He's willing and keen
But a tiny bit wonky...

"So he's not the best choice for a travelling man,
But he'll carry your lady as well as he can."
The woman was weary and ready to drop,
So she climbed on the beast
And his hoofs went clip-clop.

But since all its legs were assorted in size
Poor Mary felt sea-sick. She covered her eyes
And she tried not to groan as she wobbled about,
Though pathways were rocky,
Directions in doubt.

At last, they arrived at an Inn - shut and barred.
The donkey went: 'Hee-Haw.' He clopped round the yard,
Till the Inn-Keeper shouted: "If someone is able
To silence that donkey
I'll lend you my stable."

Well - the shelter was cosy and peace seemed to reign -
Until the daft donkey went: 'Hee-Haw' again.
He was trying to nibble the hay in the manger,
So the oxen (quite rightly)
Were nudging the stranger.

But hush ! They heard cries like a chorus of joy -
And there in the straw - lay a new baby boy !
And even the donkey grew quiet just then,
While someone above him
Sang softly: "Amen."

The Inn-Keeper's wife came with blankets and bread.
There were shepherds. And camels. And kings, it is said !
But the donkey who tried to be faithful and strong
Remembered that journey
So hard and so long...
And the smile of the mother. The angel's sweet song.

****

A LITTLE MOUSE TAIL.
****

I am the mouse
Who hides by the manger,
Nibbling crumbs in the dark. Out of danger.
The mother is quiet, her man by her side -
They gaze at their baby
With wonder and pride.

The shepherds have gone
With their whimpering hound -
Their fleeces and cheeses are scattered around.
The rich men brought caskets, then clattered away -
Leaving their tributes
To gleam in the hay.

The oxen are sleeping,
Their hoofs do not stir...
I creep from my nest with: a tangle of fur,
A strand of gold thread from the robes of a king,
A fragment of bread
And a carol to sing.

The baby is lit
By the star and the moon,
I offer my gifts and I squeak an old tune
Of love and of kindness - but down swoop the wings
As wide as an eagle's,
As deadly as stings.

I bare my sharp teeth -
And I cry: "Spare the child !
I'm small and I'm tasty - a feast warm and wild."
But voices are whispering: "Bravest and best,
Here's something to guard you
At night. In your nest."

I'll remember those words
And that baby forever...
As I curl in the fronds
Of an Angel's bright feather.

****

THE THREE WISE MICE.
****

(a.k.a. Cheddar, Mozarella and Brie.)

The Three Wise Mice, despite advice,
Set off in starry gowns
To follow dreams and
And camel teams
Through forests, fields and towns.

They nibbled wood, as Wise Mice should,
And seeds (when seeds were found).
They hid in holes
With rats and moles
When cats came prowling round.

While rich men slept, they nimbly crept
Inside a humble house,
And there they saw
In golden straw
A babe curled like a mouse.

By candle-glow they each bowed low
And offered gifts to please -
Berries red
And crumbs of bread,
Plus golden chunks of cheese.

They squeaked a spell (or so they tell)
For nestlings born to roam...
Then skipped away
As spears of day
Broke through, to guide them
Home.
****

(Inspired by Anita Jeram's charming Christmas card.)

THE INN-KEEPER'S CAT.
****

(For Mycroft - my lovely, old black cat)

Black as a curtain of shade,
In a velvet heap
In a mask of sleep
The Inn-Keeper's Tom-Cat prayed...

"Let me catch mice by the score,
From the manger hay,
From the dawn of day,
A feast on my stable floor."

Coiled where a star coldly gleamed,
By a bale of straw,
By the stable door,
The Inn-Keeper's Tom-Cat dreamed...

Light shone like ice on his fur,
On his sharpened claws,
On his hungry jaws,
He woke with a hopeful purr.

But as he sprang up from his bed,
Like a magic charm,
Like a soothing balm,
A hand touched his Tom-Cat head.

And stroking his whiskers wild,
She tamed his mind
With words so kind
He bowed to her holy child.

Now the fieldmice safely crept,
Forgetting his speed,
Forgetting his greed,
He kept them safe while they slept.

And just where the hand touched his coat,
Like a gift from a bride,
Like a token of pride,
A dazzle of frost lit his throat.

And every black cat, to this day,
With sleek feline flair,
With a white streak of hair,
Remembers that dream in the hay.

****

(If you stroke a friendly, black cat - maybe you'll spot one white hair !)

THE SPIDERS OF BETHLEHEM.
****

"Why do we scatter our tree with webs
Of spidery ribbons and silver threads ?"

The night spread a shawl of shadows
Over the bustling town;
Beasts in the stable grew sleepy
As the darkness drifted down.

A cry went up, and the creatures
Shuffled with hoof and with paw -
A child was placed in the manger,
A nestling bedded in straw.
But the Spiders climbed to a rafter,
Hidden from bat and from bird,
Webs hung in trembling tatters,
Where draughts from the doorway stirred.

Now the Spiders scuttled quickly
To spin through the dusty air,
They wove a charm for the father,
A shawl for the mother's chair.
They whirled a curtain of wishes
Where the little one quietly curled -
They stitched a pattern of moonlight
To welcome him to the world.

Stars slid away from the hillside,
The township yawned in the sun,
The Spiders crawled to their rooftop,
Knowing their labour was done.
Each thread had been strung with droplets
Like gems from a royal ring,
A sparkle of frosty diamonds,
A gift for an infant king.

The donkey woke in the stable
To stare at a homeless child -
But Joseph woke in a palace,
Where his wife and his baby smiled.

"So that's why we scatter our tree with webs
Of spidery ribbons and silver threads."

****

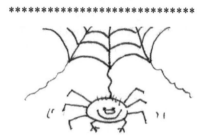

GIFTS FOR THE BABY.
****

When Mary came to the stable
She brought the wonder of birth,
The gift of a precious baby,
A present for all the Earth.

When the Inn-Keeper came to the stable
With straw for the customer's bed,
He brought the baby a welcome,
And somewhere to lay his head.

When the children came to the stable
To tickle the tiny boy,
They brought the gift of their laughter
And they filled the air with their joy.

When the shepherds came to the stable,
To gaze at the stranger's child -
They brought the fleeces of friendship,
So soft - that the baby smiled.

When the wise men came to the stable
Their gifts were more precious than gold -
Kindness and wonder and glory,
And a tale that will never grow old.

When Joseph came to the stable
He thought his gifts were too small -
But the love that he gave to the baby
Was the best Christmas present of all.

****

13

THE CHRISTMAS WREATH.
****

"What will you bring for the Christmas Wreath,
From the shimmering shops
And the frosty heath ?"

Mistletoe boughs to greet the day,
The scent of leaves, as sweet as hay.

Holly and ivy for birds to twine,
Silver foil for the stars that shine.

Golden charms for an infant king,
Leaves as bright as an angel's wing.

Twists of wool for a shepherd's prayer,
Milk-white webs for a mother's care.

Fragrant wood from a father's hand,
Fiery berries to warm the land.

A message of love for a manger bed,
And moss to cushion the baby's head.

"From the shimmering shops and the frosty heath -
These are our gifts
For the Christmas Wreath."

****

STARS OF WONDER.
****

When the shepherds ran
From a dazzle of light,
When voices followed their downward flight -
A friendly star
Made their pathway bright.

When wise men wandered
Too long, too far,
When the wind grew harsh as a battle scar,
They turned their gaze
To a patient star.

When the family fled
To a kindly town,
When tracks were steep and muddy brown -
A comforting star
Shone softly down.

When sailors dreaded
The snarling storm,
When waves rose up in a scary swarm -
A faithful star
Kept their courage warm

And when you're lost,
When your dreams fall through,
When nothing goes right, whatever you do -
Look up. Find the star
That shines
For you.
****

ONE STAR.
****

One star
Is all it takes.

Just one star
Escaping from clouds
To paint a ribbon of silver
Along the shivery edges
Of winter twigs.

One small shimmer of light
Reaching down
To touch your chilly fingers
With a spark of hope,
A promise of warmth
At the end of the darkest trail.

One sudden flash,
One wild firework of joy
Spilling its magic across the world,
Until
Your own eyes sparkle
And the kindness of Christmas
Glows and flows
In circles of comfort,
Ripples of delight.

Just one star.
May it shine for you,
Tonight.

****

CHRISTMAS AT SCHOOL

THE CHRISTMAS PLAY.
****

Here is an Inn, with a stable
Equipped with some straw and a chair:
Here is an Angel in bed-sheets,
With tinsel to tie back her hair.
Here is a Servant in bath-towels,
Who sweeps round the stage with a broom;
Here is a chorus of faces
All eager to cry out: "NO ROOM !"

Here is a Joseph who stammers
And tries to remember his lines:
Here is a Teacher in anguish,
Who frantically gestures and signs.
Here is 'Away In A Manger' -
A tune MOST recorders can play !
Here is the moment of wonder
As Jesus appears in the hay.

Here is a Mary with freckles
Whose baby is plastic and hard:
Here is a Donkey in trousers,
With ears made from pieces of card.
Here is a Shepherd in curtains,
Who carries a crook made of wire;
Here is a boy sucking cough sweets,
Who growls at the back of the Choir.

Here is a King bearing bath-salts,
Who points at a star hung on strings;
Here is a Dove who has stage-fright
And quivers her papery wings.
Here is a Page Boy in slippers
Who stumbles his way up the stairs;
And here is a long line of Angels
Who march round the manger in pairs.

Here is a Camel who fidgets
With plasters stuck over his knee:
Here are some Sheep who just giggle
And think no one out there can see.
Here is a Herod in glasses
Who whispers - so nobody hears:
Here is a Mum with a hanky
To cover her pride and her tears.

Here is our Final Production,
And though it's still held up with pins,
The parents will love every moment
For this is where Christmas begins.

MARY.

******

Ellie Jones is Mary
Which I think isn't fair -
Just because she's kind and cute
With loads of shiny hair.

Just because she's small and thin,
Just because she's quiet,
Just because the rest of us
Are LOUD and on a diet.

Just because she learns her words,
Just because she's good,
Just because she sits SO still
When people say she should.

Just because she's neat and clean,
Just because her mother
Is lending us a Jesus -
WHO
Is Ellie's baby brother.

******

JOSEPH.
****

I am Joseph
Speak my part
VERY SLOWLY
Off by heart.

Mary's tired
And shy and fat,
"GIVE US ROOM PLEASE,"
Rat-tat-tat.

I stand behind
The manger bed,
While a load of
Lines are said.

Watch the Shepherds
Lead their Sheep -
Wrapped in wool
And half asleep.

Watch the Kings
In dressing gowns,
Bending low
With royal frowns.

But Joseph is
The part for me -
Just ONE line
Then home for tea.
****

THE DONKEY.

****

I am the Donkey
Because I am strong.
I clump round the stage
While my class sings a song.

My costume is heavy
And scratchy and grey,
I can't see my feet
With this mask in the way.

I stand next to Joseph
For hours and hours -
I yawn and I fidget
While Gabriel glowers.

Then my mask sort-of slips
And my ears sort-of wiggle;
Our Teacher looks cross
But the Mums start to giggle.

So now, feeling cheerful,
I wiggle some more;
Our Teacher looks wild
But the Dads start to roar.

My ears are so happy
They're flapping like flies;
The parents are snorting
And mopping their eyes.

What's rattled our Teacher ?
My ears might be wonky -
But EVERYONE says
I'm a brilliant Donkey.

****

NO ROOM AT THE INN.
****

I've been the Inn-Keeper every year
Since I was small -
That's why you'll hear
My voice ring out as clear doom:

"NO ROOM !"

My teacher says I must learn my words
And let them soar
Like snowy birds -
I'll take a breath, I'll shake my broom:

"NO ROOM !"

My Mum (who's old, so she should know)
Says I'm the STAR
Of this year's show.
Who else can make the rafters boom ?

"NO ROOM !"

****

LITTLE ANGEL.
****

I'm always the Angel
Because of my hair -
I stand at the back
On a wobbly chair.

I'm good at rehearsals
In spotless, white clothes,
I never pull faces
Or play with my nose.

I'm still as a statue
While others perform -
But wait till the concert
And watch me transform...

I'll wave at my parents,
I'll fidget and lurch,
I'll scratch all my itches,
I'll slide off my perch.

I'll whisper my speeches,
I'll sniff and forget !
I'll drop my recorder,
I'll giggle...and yet

When everyone stands
In a group round the tree -
All of the papers
Will photograph
ME !
****

A Star Is Born !

THE SHEPHERD.

****

I'm a boring Shepherd
In the boring crowd,
With a boring line
That I shout out LOUD !

There's a boring wait
When the whole class sings,
While the boring girls
Flap their boring wings.

There's a boring gasp
When I point my crook,
At a boring star
On a boring hook.

There's a boring walk
Round the baby's bed,
With a boring towel
On my boring head.

It's a boring part,
And it's VERY small...
But
Good old Gran and Grandad
Don't seem bored
AT ALL !

****

THE SHEEP.

****

We're the sheep.........................Baa ! Baa !

Learned our lines..........................Blah ! Blah !

Woolly jumpers........................Ha ! Ha !

Made us itch................................Waa ! Waa !

Sang our song.........................Tra ! La !

Skipped about..............................Cha ! Cha !

Tripped downstairs............................Oooh ! Aaaah !

Nudged the camel....................Ya ! Ya !

Waved and grinned....................Grandma !

End of show................................Tan - Tara !

Took a bow...............................Hoo - rah !

Home to bed..........................Ta ! Ta !

Counting sheep............................Baa ! Baa !...

BAAAAAAAAAAAAAAAA !

****

26

THE LITTLE DRUMMER BOY.

****

There's a drummer on the doorstep !
There's a drummer ! With a drum !
He says he's brought a present
For the Baby and his Mum.
He says his drum is magic
When we want our son to sleep -
He says his drum is better than
A flock of jumping sheep

But the noise is growing louder
(Though we've stuffed our ears with straw)
And all the grumpy shepherds
Have gone home - and slammed the door.
While the angels with their haloes
Have begun to flap away.
And the oxen all have headaches,
And the donkey starts to BRAY !

And Mary's looking tearful,
And the Keeper of the Inn
Says we'll have to leave tomorrow
If we can't control the din !
And the baby starts to whimper,
And my head beats like a gong...
And NOW the wretched drummer
Says he'll sing
A little song.

****

(To be followed by the children singing: 'The Little Drummer Boy'.)

SHINE ON.
****

Most years - I just stand
At the back of the stage,
Too thin for a Shepherd,
Too tall for a Page,
Too shy to be Herod -
Can't bellow. Or rage.

I once was a Cow
Which was easy to play -
I wore a large mask
And had NOTHING to say...
Apart from the moment
I MOOED at the hay.

But this year - guess what ?
I'm the Star of the Show !
I'm all dressed in gold
So I'm certain to GLOW
When I stand on my spot
And a Teacher says: 'GO !'

Then I flicker my torch
And the Kings point and stare
As I light up a pathway
Of starlight to where...
The Angels are flapping
Their arms and their hair.

I don't have to sing
And I don't have to shout,
I don't need to jingle
Or scamper about.
I just have to SHINE -
And our Teachers don't doubt
I will brighten their lives...

Till my battery runs out !

****

←Me.

PAGE - BOY PROTEST.
****

Our teacher likes to use us all,
So when we act our play
Everybody gets a part
(If not a line to say).

At Christmas, there are Shepherds,
While shy ones are their flocks,
The Inn is kept by someone LOUD
In sandals (but no socks).

The sweet ones are the Angels
With long and wavy hair,
The naughty ones have padded humps
Or Donkey masks to wear.

Mary is a quiet child,
A cheerful boy is Joe,
The oldest are the Three Wise Men -
Which leaves one group to go.

We stamp around the platform
Embarrassingly dressed,
In baggy pants and turbans...
It's no wonder we protest.

I know we're rather tiny,
With hair that never curls
BUT
This year, let's get one thing straight -
We're not Page-Boys.
We're GIRLS.
****

← My Hat!

HEROD.
****

I didn't want to be Herod.
I thought the parents would BOO !
I thought the other children
Would start to hate me too.

I thought my friends would vanish
And leave me all alone.
I thought I'd spend my playtimes
In a corner, on my own.

So, when the Kings came calling
And they pointed at a star,
I said: "I know that stable.
It isn't very far."

The hall went strangely silent
As I led them past the cattle.
I bowed my knee to Mary
And I handed her a rattle.

Of course, my poor old Henchmen
Couldn't wave their knives -
But that's a tiny price to pay
For saving brand new lives.

I thought perhaps our teacher
Would shout at me and scold...
But all she did was blow her nose !
Maybe she's caught a cold ?

And when we sang our carol
To end our Christmas Play,
I THINK the parents liked me -
(Well, mine did anyway).

****

THE THIRD KING.

****

We three Kings
Have gifts to hold -
Simon's parcel
Shines like gold.
Sunil's giving
Frankincense
In a jar that's
Just IMMENSE !
Mine's a cake-tin,
Wrapped by Sir,
"Lo ! I bring a
Box of Myrrh."

Gold is useful,
No doubt there.
Frankincense
Can scent the air.
But surely Mary
Would prefer
ANY sort of gift
But Myrrh ?

Babies need the
Kind of things
Never given
By the Kings.
Teddies, bunnies,
Tiny hats,
Woolly vests,
Or changing mats,
Little clothes
As soft as fur,
SO
Why on earth
Have I brought
MYRRH ?

****

JUST DOING MY JOB.
****

I'm one of Herod's Henchmen.
We don't have much to say,
We just charge through the audience
In a Henchman sort of way.

We all wear woolly helmets
To hide our hair and ears,
And wellingtons sprayed silver
To match our tinfoil spears.

Our swords are made of cardboard
So blood will not be spilled
If we trip and stab a parent
When the hall's completely filled.

We don't look VERY scary -
We're mostly small and shy,
And some of us wear glasses,
But we give the thing a try.

We whisper Henchmen noises
While Herod hunts for strangers,
And then we all charge out again
Like frightened Power-Rangers.

Yet, when the play is over
And Miss is out of breath...
We'll CHARGE like Henchmen
Through the hall
And scare our Mums to death.
****

THE CHRISTMAS DOVE.
****

I am the Dove
With my white paper wings -
I flutter and twirl
While the Angel Band sings.

But first, they're too fast,
Then they puff and they blow,
Till I'm not in the place
Where the Dove's meant to go.

So I flap round the manger
To reach the right spot,
But I bump into Joseph
Who grumbles - a lot !

He gives me a shove
(Which is NOT very holy)
I twitter. I wobble.
I tumble quite slowly...

And land on the Camel
Who's wobbling too -
I've unstuck his humps
Which took AGES to glue.

She's out for revenge
So she bashes a wing,
And that's when I crash
Into Herod the King.

He PINGS the elastic
Attached to my beak,
So I let out a SQUAWK
As the Mice sadly squeak:

"The Message of Christmas
Is brought by our Dove -
We wish you a season
Of Peace
And of LOVE."

****

I REALLY WOULD LIKE TO BE MARY.
****

I really would like to be Mary -
The very best part in the play.
I could sit by the crib with my baby,
Centre stage ! With nothing to say !

I wouldn't mind being an Angel
With wings and a halo that shines.
I could stand at the back looking holy,
And memorise everyone's lines.

I wouldn't mind being a Snowflake
With tinsel pinned over my hair;
Or a Page-Boy with myrrh on a cushion,
And a tea-cosy turban to wear.

I wouldn't mind being a Robin,
With a patch of red stuck to my chest;
Or a Camel wrapped up in a blanket,
With a bulge in the back of my vest.

I wouldn't mind being Narrator,
Provided the words weren't too long:
Or the person who crashes the cymbals
When we come to the end of our song.

I wouldn't mind selling the programmes -
No, any old part would suit me...
SO
Can anyone answer my question ?
Why is it I'm ALWAYS a tree ?

THE INFANTS' NATIVITY PLAY.
****
(Or: The Key-Ring And The Waiter.)

I am the Key-Ring and Josie's the Waiter,
No one knows why
But we might find out later.

Our Mums want to know what on earth we should wear...
Our Teacher says ANYTHING,
She doesn't care
As long as we're all looking merry and bright,
And we smile at the crowd
On Nativity night.

Our Mums start to grumble - We should have been Kings,
Or Shepherds. Or Angels
With twinkly wings.
But Josie's dressed up in a Waitressy frock,
And I have a necklace
Of Keys. With a Lock !

Our Mums take their seats in the front - so we wave !
(Well, that's how a Waiter
And Key-Ring behave.)
BUT
Josie's been given a story to tell,
And I'm in the Band
With a jingly bell ?

So Josie turns round - and she whispers to me:
"Maybe we aren't
What we THOUGHT we would be !"
And the Play's going well as I DING and I DONG,
Then Josie reads LOUDLY,
We all sing our song...

And our Mums are SO happy, they smile at Miss Stringer -
Now Josie's NARRATOR
And I'm the BELL-RINGER.

****

(For Rachael.)

A CHRISTMAS COUNTDOWN.
****

TEN...Tired Teachers - Who whimper and rage.

NINE...Dancing Donkeys - Who fall off the stage.

EIGHT...Awful Angels - With horrible habits.

SEVEN...Red Robins - Who scamper like rabbits.

SIX...Singing Snowflakes - Who never stop sneezing.

FIVE...Scratchy Snowmen - Whose costumes have fleas in.

FOUR...Flappy Fairies - With wobbly wings.

THREE...Precious Presents - From giggly Kings.

TWO...Frightened Fir Trees - Too quiet. Too slow.

AND

ONE...Truly Typical - End-Of-Term Show !

****

CHRISTMAS CATASTROPHE.
****

It was Christmas again in the classroom,
And time for the annual play.
The costumes were just about finished,
The props would be right on the day.

The actors were almost word-perfect,
And EVERYONE knew what to do:
It seemed that our scene was a winner -
Then along came an outbreak of flu !

The Partridge was fine (when not sneezing),
As she staggered around with her tree;
The Doves croaked their lines between coughing;
The French Hens were TWO and not THREE.

The Calling Birds mimed with their feathers;
But only ONE ring could be found;
The Geese said their eggs made them queasy;
And half of the Swans must have drowned.

The Maids did their milking in relays,
While the two-legged Cow stole the show;
The Drummers stayed home with sick headaches;
And the Pipers brought hankies to blow.

The Ladies made quite a nice circle,
Considering TEN couldn't come;
But as for just TWO Lords-a-Leaping...
They limped round the stage looking glum.

We won't have this trouble in future.
The flu-bug has had its last fling...
Oh, we'll still have our Festive Performance -
But we won't put it on
Till the SPRING.
****

40

OUR GRUMPY OLD CARETAKER.
****

Our grumpy old Caretaker glares up and down -
With speckled green eyes
And a grumpy old frown

He glares at our Classroom. He glares at our books.
He glares at our drawings
With speckled green looks.
He glares at our snowflakes. He glares at our trees.
He glares at the paint
On our tables and knees.

He glares at the roof when he hunts for a ball,
He glares at the Carols
We sing in the hall...

And I'm SURE that he doesn't like children AT ALL !

****

The Santa who visits our school's Christmas Fair,
Is too big and merry
To grumble and glare.

His questions are gentle. His laughter is kind.
He listens with patience -
Takes AGES to find
The very best gift from his sackful of toys,
With never a frown
For the girls. Or the boys.

His jokes are so funny. His clothes are so bright.
His smile is so jolly.
His beard is so white...

And I'm SURE that our Santa thinks kids are ALL RIGHT !

****

(But just as I'm leaving - it's quite a surprise
To notice Old Santa
Has speckled green eyes.)

****

THE CAROL SINGER'S STORY.

****

I thought it was Good King Wences.
That's how it seemed to me...
'Good King Wences LAST looked out.'
Obviously.

Perhaps he was feeling dizzy.
Perhaps he was sick of snow.
Perhaps he'd lost his spectacles -
We'll never know.

Perhaps I should say I'm sorry,
But 'Wences' just sounds fine -
So you can sing your boring words
And I'll sing MINE.

****

THE CAROL SINGER'S CONFESSION.

****

They tell me my singing is painful -
It sounds like the twanging of wire,
Or finger nails scratching a white-board...
And now I've been sacked from the choir.

They told me I shouldn't try singing;
They told me I'd ruin their day;
But look ! I've collected fortune
In bribes...just to keep me away !
****

THE CHRISTMAS CHOIR.

****

(To be sung to the tune of: 'Good King Wenceslas.')

Good King Wences...Pom-te-Pom,
Both my feet are freezing,
Ben has got an awful cold,
I can hear him wheezing.
Brightly shone the...Dum-de-Dum,
Mo and Jo are fighting,
No one seems to know the words
And the wind is Bi-i-Ting.

Hither page and ...Da-de-Da,
Wish I had my vest on,
Wish I had a blow-up bed
I could take a rest on.
Sire he lives a...Rum-te-Tee,
I can smell the Chip Shop.
Sammy's singing out of tune -
Someone pass a co-ough-drop.

Bring me flesh and...Do-ray-Me,
This is where my friend lives,
Sing the next line TWICE AS LOUD,
Let's see what his Mum gives.
Page and Monarch...Fee-fi-Fum,
Now my nose is runny,
Never mind. It's time to stop...
Let's share out the Mo-o-ney.

****

ANOTHER CHRISTMAS CAROL !

****

(For a year when there's no snow - just boring rain !)

To be sung to the tune of: 'In The Bleak Mid-Winter.'

****

IN THE WET MID-WINTER.

****

In the wet mid-winter,
Poor old Granny moans:

"I've got leaky wellies
I've got creaky bones.

Water swirls around my bed
Where my slippers float,

All I want for Christmas
Is
A Motor-Boat !"

****

A CHRISTMAS QUESTION.
****

What's the matter with our Teachers
Now Christmas time is here ?
The most exciting month at school
In all the boring year !

Our pictures just need paint and glue,
And spiky stars to scatter -
So, if we spill a blob or two
It really doesn't matter.
There's cotton wool in happy heaps
For smudgy, snowy scenes,
And paper-chains to lick and stick -
Since THAT'S what Christmas means.

There are Carols to be practised
With recorders round the tree,
And cymbals to be clashed (and dropped)
Which sounds like fun to me.
There are costumes to be rescued
From the cupboards in the hall,
With droopy wings and turbans,
Plus the manger (straw and all) .

There are words to be remembered,
For our Merry Christmas Show -
We say them very soft and fast,
Or very LOUD and slow.
There are parts to be invented
(So NOBODY'S left out)...
Mice and flocks of singing sheep
Or trees who skip about.

There are parties to be organised
Instead of silent sums -
Children full of chocolate cake
And floors knee-deep in crumbs.
SO
What's upset our Teachers,
Why DO they look so glum ?
Just because they've all caught colds
Now Christmas time has come.

****

(AAAAACHOO !)

****

In the dark days of Winter - all around the World, people love to brighten their
streets, homes and meeting places with candles, bonfires, fireworks and fairy-lights.

(Bonfire Night, Eid Mubarak, Guru Nanak's Birthday, Hanukkah, Chinese New Year - and many more.)

This poem is about a happy celebration called Diwali.

****

RAINBOW RICE.

****

When Arzana came to school today
She wore silky robes
That smelled of spices
And excitement.

She spoke of candle-flames
And fireworks
That still sparkled in her eyes,
And she brought us bowls
Of rainbow-coloured rice
Tasting of sugar
And sweet surprises.

I shall forget the dates
Of kings and queens
And far-off battles.
I shall forget the names
Of tiny islands
In shimmering seas.
A thousand facts will slip from my mind
Like scuttling mice.

But years from now,
When I am no longer young
The tingle of Arzana's rainbow rice
Will always be
On the tip of my tongue.

****

And finally: a grumpy School Inspector who has forgotten about
nasty bugs...

POOR MISS SNIFF.
****

The Chief Inspector glared around,
He raged, he fumed, he growled, he frowned.

"Miss Sniff," he snarled with angry sneers,
"Why are fingers stuffed in ears ?
And why the chaos ? Why the seizing
Shields and helmets ? What's the reason
For your masks ? And metal suits ?
Waterproofs and rubber boots ?"

The classroom door stood open wide,
The winter weather sneaked inside,
The atmosphere grew fierce and freezing -
And suddenly Miss Sniff was
SNEEZING !

We didn't peep. We didn't dare.
A dreadful roaring filled the air,
The windows rattled, pictures shook,
The whiteboard swung upon its hook,
A tidal wave of sound came lashing,
Tables tumbled, glass went smashing...

The Chief Inspector lost his hat,
His nasty notebook (big and fat),
His brand new wig, his tie so grey -
And with a YELP
He blew away !

While poor Miss Sniff
(Who's kind and old)
Said:
"Sorry dear.
I've caught a cold."

****

CHRISTMAS AT HOME

**********************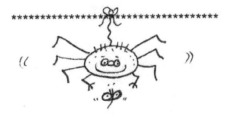**********************

SAUCE FOR THE GOOSE.

****

"I'm fed up with turkey,"
Said Grandad last Spring,
"Let's go for tradition !
A goose is the thing.
There's plenty of dripping
And plenty of meat,
Plus plenty of feathers -
A seasonal treat."

So...

We bought a fine gander
And fattened him up
With barley and biscuits
And bread from a cup.
He lived in our garden
And slept in our shed.
We called him Goliath
And tickled his head.

He chased off intruders,
He guarded our gate,
And no one dared mention
His terrible fate.
But Christmas drew closer
As Christmases will -
Goliath grew fatter
While Grandad grew ill...

He no longer wanted
To cook his best friend,
It gave him goose-pimples
To think of the end.
Well,

We all loved Goliath,
But what could we do ?
We had him for Christmas
And Boxing Day too -

He sat at our table
As proud as could be,
And shared Grandad's dinner
And shared Grandad's tea !

****

(A Gander is a Mister Goose.)

CHRISTMAS TREE CAT.

****

The cat up the tree
Is confused as can be
By garlands that trap the unwary.
Then the pot starts to sway
In a worrying way
Till her yowls are incredibly scary !

Our star has been scragged
And the branches have sagged,
The lovely glass baubles are hairy...
Then the lightbulbs go POP
As she clings to the top
BUT
At least it's a change
From the Fairy.

****

POT PLANT POEM.

****

We gave Mum a pot plant,
A brilliant red,
To brighten our Christmas -
That's what the shop said.

But now it's gone droopy
And brown to upset us...
Next year, we'll have sense
And we'll stick to a cactus.

****

(The posh name for this red plant is a Poinsettia,)

OUR BAY TREE.
****

Your sky-rocket trees
Bought from heaps on the ground
Are tall, proud and pointy...
But OUR tree is round !

It lives by our lawn
In a pot of red clay,
Not a Pine. Not a Fir - Our tree is a Bay.
It stands in the sun,
Or the rain if it pours,
But just around Christmas - Our tree comes indoors.

A circular tree
On a lollipop stick -
And though it sounds silly - Our tree does the trick.
We drape its green leaves
In a silver disguise,
And though it sounds loopy - Our tree takes the prize.

We paper the pot
And we tie a red bow,
And though it sounds foolish - Our tree seems to know.
It watches our fun,
And whatever we do,
The day seems complete - When our tree sits there too.

But after Twelfth Night,
If there's rain, hail or snow,
The party is over - Our tree has to go.
We strip off the stars
As the ribbons unweave,
Then unwrap the pot - And our tree has to leave.

It stands looking in
At the window all day -
But what it is thinking
Our tree will not say...

BIRD TABLE BLUES.
****

In Winter, Grandma feeds the birds
With kindly thoughts and friendly words...

And biscuit crumbs, and broken baps,
And bacon rinds, and breakfast scraps,
And plates of freshly buttered toast,
And bags of chips, and Sunday roast,
And dumplings (huge and hot and steamy),
And home-made pies, and gravy (creamy),
And every sort of cheese and bread,
Until each hungry bird is fed...

To BURSTING point, to bitter end,
Until their legs begin to bend,
Until they cannot flap or fly,
Until they simply want to die,
Until they roll around the floor
And weakly twitter: "Stop ! No more !"

Then Grandma smiles and says:
"Oh good !
I think they're ready for their pud."

****

CRUMBS OF COMFORT.
****

A small bird flew out of the shivering wood,
She was longing for shelter and dreaming of food.
Her spirit was broken, her body was weak,
And she ached for the comfort
Of scraps in her beak.

So she searched every lawn for a seed or a nut,
But curtains were drawn and the kitchens were shut.
At last, in despair and with faltering sighs,
She clung to a willow
And blinked her sad eyes.

****

An old woman sat by her fireside alone,
Her mind full of memories. Heart cold as stone.
She stared at the pictures that smiled on her shelf
But those voices had gone,
So she wept by herself.

Her cake lay untouched on its blue china plate.
She crumbled it sadly, and whispered: "Too late."
Then, dragging her feet with a shuffling sound,
She opened her door,
Threw the crumbs on the ground.

****

Once more, in her room, she reached for her chair...
When suddenly music was filling the air !
For a small bird who sat in the willow outside
Sang a song of the hope
That so nearly had died.

Now happiness changed that old house to a home !
The bird and the woman were no more alone...
Their friendship brought joy for very long while -
The bird found a friend -
And the woman
Her smile.

****

A CHRISTMAS ACROSTIC.

****

Cakes rich with currants now Christmas has come;

Helpings of trifle, home-made by Mum;

Rows of roast chestnuts that suddenly POP;

Icing so scrummy I simply can't stop;

Snowmen meringues wearing marzipan hats;

Titbits of turkey to feed to the cats;

Mince pies to munch and biscuits to bite;

Apples to crunch and treats to delight;

Sweets from our stockings...I'm full up ! Good night.

****

If you look down the left side of this delicious poem - you should spot

CHRISTMAS !!

****

61

THE CHOCOLATE LOG.
****

(For Martin.)

There is only ONE way to eat a chocolate log -
My way.
It goes like this.

First, you pull out the robin, or the sprig of holly,
Or whatever,
And very, very, slowly
You nibble the gooey stuff off the spike.

Then you hold the roll in both hands,
Revolve it,
And very, very gently
You stick out your lips
To pick off the outside layer of chocolate
Bit by scrummy bit,
Like an edible jigsaw
Until all the parts are missing.

Now, you put the bald cake to one side,
Lick your finger
And very, very neatly
Hoover up all the crumbs
Especially the squashy ones.

After a long and thoughtful pause,
You start to unroll the cake and feed it
Very, very carefully into your mouth
LIke a creamy conveyer belt
Until all you have left
Is one yummy, oozy swirl
That very, very slowly melts on your tongue.

Finally,
You hide your holly, or robin, or whatever
In your pocket,
Lift up your spotless, shiny plate and say:
"Any chocolate cake left
For me
Today ?"

****

A REALLY GOOD PARTY.

****

I didn't win Musical Parcels,
I dropped out of Musical Chairs...

I wriggled in Musical Statues,
I sneezed when I hid on the stairs.

I didn't pin tails on the Reindeer;
I didn't solve Puzzles for fun;

I didn't draw jolly old Snowmen;
I couldn't solve Clues (one-by-one);

I couldn't find ANY lost Slippers;
I couldn't quite Spot-The-Mistake;

In fact, I was totally rubbish -
BUT
I did eat THREE helpings of cake.

****

THE CHRISTMAS CRIMINAL.
****

Who stole our Christmas Pudding ?
Who swiped our Christmas Day Pud ?
Surely it couldn't be Santa ?
(Though he DOES have a sack and a hood.)

Who stole our Christmas Pudding,
Then ran off with ALL the mince pies ?
Surely it wasn't our Fairy
With her innocent, glittery eyes ?

Who stole our Christmas Pudding,
The pies and the snacks - the whole pile ?
Surely it wasn't our Snowman,
With his two twiggy hands. And his smile ?

Who stole our Christmas Pudding,
The pies and the snacks AND the cake ?
Surely it couldn't be Rudolph ?
That's a SHOCKING suggestion to make !

So WHO stole our Christmas Pudding,
Our treats and our trifle for tea ?

It wasn't the Maids (who were milking);
Or the Partridge (who sits in the tree);
The Hens and the Geese (who were laying);
The Swans (who swam over the sea);
The Dog (who just snored in his basket);
The Cat (who was kicking a flea);
Or even a Gang of Red Robins,
(I think they'd be easy to see),
And it couldn't be Gran...
Wait a minute -

Why is EVERYONE staring at ME ?
****

65

BABY'S FIRST CHRISTMAS.
****

There's a cracker in the cat-flap,
There's a Fairy in the sink -
And someone's torn the tinsel off the wall.
The Christmas cards have scattered
Like a flock of startled birds
To decorate the carpet in the hall.

There is chaos in the kitchen,
There is custard mixed with sprouts,
There are smears of mashed-up carrot on the door.
There's a rather festive pattern
That's a bit like chocolate stars
On the boiler and the cupboards and the floor.

There's a teddy in the trifle,
There's a shoe in Grandad's soup,
There's a rattle where the serving spoon should go.
There's a blob of something nasty
On the cloth we keep for best
And the candle (now it's nibbled) cannot glow.

There's a tortured cry of horror
As an ancient lump of rusk
Is found inside the bowl of cheesy snacks.
There's a less-than-joyful outburst
From an Aunty on the stairs
Who's trodden on a duck that really quacks.

While the cause of all the trouble
Sits enchanted by the tree
His baby-mind too full to want for dinner -
With a strip of well-chewed ribbon
And a dented cardboard box,
He's already voted Christmas Day a winner !

****

(Or the baby might be a girl !)

THE ANGEL TEST.

****

"Be an Angel," Mother said,
As she tucked me up in bed."

But Angels are such PERFECT things -
Golden haloes. Shiny wings.
I'd have to try my very best
To pass my Mother's
Tricky Test !

I tied some ribbons round my hair,
I found a floaty skirt to wear -
And fairy-wings (too small, too blue)
But never mind.
They'd have to do.

I quickly climbed my bedside table,
I flapped as fast as I was able.
I jumped and bumped.
I THUMPED some more -
My parents thundered through the door
And found an ANGEL
On the floor.

"All I wanted," Mother wailed,
"Was perfect peace."

I think I failed.

****

THE FALLEN ANGEL.
****

Our cat has caught an Angel
And we don't know what to do.

An Angel ?
In our humble home ?
It's crazy - but it's true.
She's underneath our table
And her wings have gone askew,

We've found a friendly shoebox
Which is welcoming and airy,
And yet she hasn't looked at it -
Perhaps she thinks it's scary.

But wait a minute.
Silly me !
She's just our
Christmas Fairy.

****

THE CHRISTMAS FAIRY'S SONG.

****

When you plant your Christmas Tree
Decorate it lovingly,
Pin each sparkly star with care -
I'll be hiding,
I'll be there.

When you twist your tinsel strands,
Sprinkle glitter from your hands,
Comb your Fairy's silky hair,
I'll be watching,
I'll be there.

When you find, on Christmas Day,
Bulgy stockings, games to play,
Books and toys and sweets to share
I'll be dancing,
I'll be there.

When you wonder what, or who
Made your secret wish come true ?
When Christmas magic fills the air -
I'll be smiling,
I'll be there.

****

THE YEAR WE LOST OUR CHRISTMAS FAIRY.

****

We searched the box of baubles,
We peered around inside,
But we couldn't find our Fairy
However hard we tried.

We made a star of cardboard
To sparkle in her place,
But our little tree looked lonely
Without her friendly face.

Next morning, very early,
We crept downstairs to see
If Santa Claus had hidden
Any presents by the tree.

And there we saw our Fairy
Smiling down at us once more !
But lovelier than ever
In the brand new dress she wore.

We don't know how she got there,
We don't know where she'd been -
But we keep her like a treasure
And we treat her like a Queen.

****

CHRISTMAS CARD QUESTIONNAIRE.

****

Who wants a Cool card ?
A Rock-and-Rolling Yule card ?
A 'Rapping-Reindeer Rule' card ?
Not for me.

Who wants a Cute card ?
A Robin-in-a-Suit card ?
A Cat-in-Santa's-Boot card ?
Please not me.

Who wants a Snowy card ?
A Glitter-and-a-Glowy card ?
A Breezy-and-a-Blowy card ?
PLEASE not me.

Who wants a Jolly card ?
Pop-out sprigs of Holly card ?
Squeaky, singing Dolly card ?
NO. Not me.

Who wants a Square card ?
A fluffy Polar Bear card ?
A Penguin-in-a-Chair card ?
Still not me.

Who wants a Red card ?
A Santa tucked in Bed card ?
Reindeer round a Shed card ?
Maybe me ?

Who wants a Funny card ?
Snowman on a Sunny card ?
LOTS of Christmas Money card ?
ME ! ME ! ME !

****

POOR OLD POSTMAN.

****

(Or 'Postie !)

Poor old Postman
In the snow,
Christmas chilblains
On each toe.

Poor old Postman
In the rain,
Christmas blisters,
Christmas pain.

Poor old Postman,
There he goes,
Christmas tissues
At his nose.

Poor old Postman
Is it fair ?
Christmas twinges
Everywhere...

Christmas elbow,
Christmas knee -
Just to bring
Some cards to
ME !

****

OUR POSTMAN.

****

Our Postman is a Tortoise,
He's steady but he's slow !
That's why our Summer postcards come
When streets are white as snow.

That's why our Christmas cards arrive
When Spring is in the air -
That's why we've given him the sack
And swapped him for a Hare !

****

A FEW CHRISTMAS LETTERS...

THE LITTLE MOUSE.
****

Dear Father Kriss-Mouse,
Bring me, please -
Some crumbs of cake and scraps of cheese.
Or tasty crusts
Of buttered bread,
So all my children can be fed...

A secret mouse-hole
Warm and dry,
Where neither cats nor children pry.

Then pass a law
Throughout the land -
On Kriss-Mouse Day
ALL TRAPS ARE BANNED !

****

THE BIG, BAD CAT.
****

Dear Santa Claws - Send me
A mouse...or two ?
A door that will close
When I wriggle through,
Then open again
When I change my mind;
Plus a friendly human,
Who's good and kind.

I'll also want a comfy lap,
Whenever I choose to take a nap.
Some bottomless bowls
Of tasty things,
Like tiny fish
And chicken wings.
And don't forget some wool to shred -
Or else I'll tangle
Your beard instead !

****

(More Christmas Letters...)

THE HOPEFUL DOG.
****

Dear Santa Paws,
I'd love to own
A massive, meaty MONSTER bone...
A string of sausages to munch;
A slipper for my teeth to crunch;
A collar (spiked)
To show I'm tough;
A fluffy blanket
(Not too rough);
A line of trees;
A postman's leg;
Someone to pat me when I beg;
And more than ALL the stuff I've said:
A space for me
On my Owner's bed.

****

THE GOLDFISH.
****

Dear Santa Jaws,
I'd love some more...
Rainbow gravel for my floor;
A sprinkle of bugs for me to eat;
A painted mermaid
Small and sweet;
A model shipwreck - make that two.
Some plastic weeds. A change of view.
A hiding place,
And one last wish...
A rather lovely Lady Fish !

****

THE SPIDER'S WISH-LIST.
****

The Spider in the bathroom wove a heavy-duty thread,
From the nozzle of the shower
To the light bulb overhead.
And all along the webbing, she hung her stockings out -
Spider Claws would come tonight
She knew, without a doubt.

In thin and scrawly writing - She wrote eight tiny lists,
Attached with care and cunning
And with sticky, silver twists:
'A purple fly. A golden bug. A centipede. A flea.
A wasp. A moth. A beetle...
And
A special treat for ME.'

She snuggled in the centre of her web, so fine and neat,
And listened in the moonlight
For the sound of spider-feet -
And there ! Straight up the plughole, a Santa-Spider crawled
With a silky sack of parcels
Which he tugged and heaved and hauled.

"Dear Santa !
You have found me where I dangle high above,
You have granted ALL my wishes -
You're my Hero and my Love !"
But the Scarlet Santa vanished in an instant - ran away !
So our Spider lost her dinner
And her Hero's safe -
Hooray !

****

(The horrible truth - Lady Spiders often eat their husbands !)

A Message From:

THE CHRISTMAS CROW.

****

The Sparrows sing of Santa Caws
When winter blizzards blow -
He rides the skies on glossy wings
The hooded Christmas Crow.

He circles every hedge and roof
In every wood or town -
He visits all the tiny birds
Who roost when night swoops down.

In every nest he leaves a gift -
A shiny bottle top,
A beetle or a silver coin
(The sort a child might drop).

And once, a Mother Robin woke
To find a golden thread
Just bright enough to weave a crown
To fit a baby's head.

The Sparrows sing a thousand songs,
But this is all I know -
Who rides the skies on Christmas Eve ?
Old Santa Caws,
The Crow.

****

A CHRISTMAS CALAMITY.
****

I'm all in a muddle,
My life's in a mess -
I forgot to give Santa my name and address !

I wrote him a note,
From my window it flew...
Away went my list - and my hopes vanished too.

I asked for a bike
And a kite and a train,
But Rudolph won't land on my rooftop again.

So children in China
Will play with my treats;
Someone in France will be eating my sweets.

Some boys on a beach
Will unwrap my warm coat;
A child in the desert will stare at my boat.

A Grandad in Fiji
Will find my warm scarf;
A Granny will open my Joke Book - and LAUGH !

A prince will discover
My pants-in-a-box;
A penguin will pounce on my boring blue socks.

A Dragon will sniff
At a T-Shirt to wear -
And a Creature from Venus will cuddle my bear !

But as for myself,
I'll have nothing at all -
Not even a book or a bat and a ball.

Not ONE single present
To keep for my own...

I'm off to send Santa a text on the phone !

****

DEAR SANTA.
****

Dear Santa -
The world's in a terrible state.
Pollution and poverty. Hunger and hate.
The icebergs are melting,
The rain-forests burn,
There seems to be sorrow
Wherever we turn -

The creatures are dying,
The tigers, the bears,
While everyone worries
But nobody cares...
Or at least - not enough
To cry: "Stop !" and "No more !"
What's all this grabbing
And greediness for ?

So here is my Wish-List
For Christmas this year -
Bring one magic day
Without fury or fear;
One magic day when
There's no need to fight,
A day when our leaders
Put everything right.

And maybe - just maybe
The habit will grow.
We'll stop being selfish
And angry...and so
Forgiveness and friendship
And joy will increase,
And our New Year will start
With an outbreak of
PEACE.
****

THE THIEF IN THE SHOP.
****

(This is based on a TRUE story !
The naughty man saw himself on the News...)

The Thief in the Shop
Saw the gifts on the tree,
Glittery parcels, donated for free,
And intended for children with little. Or less.
Whose parents were poor
And whose lives were a mess.

The Thief in the Shop
With a sniff and a sneer
Grabbed a great handful. Why not ? They were here,
Unguarded, uncounted - and paid for by fools.
The Camera watched him
Reject Christmas Rules.

The Thief in the Shop
Soon appeared on T.V. -
His face was too hooded and hazy to see.
He couldn't be captured or given a name -
But he saw his OWN actions
And shuddered with shame.

The Thief in the Shop
In his hood (as before)
Returned all the gifts - plus a whole sackful more !
The Camera watched with a wise, patient eye
As a kindlier man
Waved a grateful 'Good bye.'

****

THE CHRISTMAS SHOE-BOX.
****

We're filling up a shoebox
For an orphan far away -
So we've bought a pile of presents
Just for him, on Christmas Day.
(And I want stacks of gadgets;
And a set of full-size drums;
And a game for my computer,
Just for me, when Christmas comes).

We've packed inside the shoebox
A flannel and some soap,
And a toothbrush, plus some toothpaste,
Which should cheer him up, I hope.
(And I want robot creatures;
And a headlamp that will glow;
And a sledge that's painted silver
For our races in the snow).

We've also put a pencil
And a ruler in his box,
And I'm sure he'll be delighted
When he sees his brand new socks.
(And I want flashy trainers;
And a bicycle with style;
And books and sweets and puzzles;
And some cash to make me smile).

There's a yo-yo and a lolly
And a little plastic ball,
And a car I used to play with -
But it isn't much at all.
(And now I want to tell him
That I'm sorry life's unfair...

And I hope his day is happy,
And
I hope he knows I care)

****

MUST - HAVE.
****

What are the MUST-HAVES, this bright Christmas Day ?
We MUST-HAVE a laptop that's slinky and grey.

We MUST-HAVE the latest in films and in games.
We MUST-HAVE a Panto with Villains and Dames.

We MUST-HAVE a robot that's programmed to fight.
Mum MUST-HAVE novels to read, late at night.

Dad MUST-HAVE gadgets. And Gran MUST-HAVE sweets.
Even old Scruff MUST-HAVE small, doggy treats.

As for the table - we MUST-HAVE mince pies;
We MUST-HAVE the crackers, with jokes and a prize;

We MUST-HAVE the gravy, the sprouts and the stuffing;
We MUST-HAVE it all. And we MUST leave out NOTHING.

But what if we CAN'T-HAVE the things on our list ?
Won't we feel gloomy when something is missed ?

Or will we be happy - when (heavens-above)
We share what we DO-HAVE ?
Our laughter
And
LOVE.

****

86

PARENT PUZZLE.
****

Something's happened to my parents -
They always USED to be
Really rather sensible
But NOW - they've brought a tree
And stuck it in our living room
So it's watching our T.V.

Something's happened to my parents -
They always USED to say:
"We must be neat and tidy,
So we'll put the toys away."
But NOW - they've dangled garlands !
They're in everybody's way,
And the carpet's full of glitter
Which I think is here to stay.

Something's happened to my parents,
They never USED to do
Lots of strange and silly things -
But NOW - (it's sad but true)
They whisper and they giggle
Which is RUDE - and naughty too.
And on the highest wardrobe
I know that someone threw
A scooter and a Noah's Ark,
All shiny-bright and new...
But WHO would hide a Robot
In the cupboard by the Loo ?

Something's happened to my parents -
I think they're having FUN !
They're pulling crackers, telling jokes
And smiling like the sun...
There's a stocking, full of presents -
And it seems to weigh a ton !
Mum says it came from Santa Claus,
So Christmas has begun ...
And then we hug and laugh and
SHOUT:
"God bless us. Everyone."

****

STICK 'EM UP.
****

Sticky tape stuck to my fingers,

Sticky tape stuck to my chair,

Sticky tape stuck to my eyebrows,

Sticky tape stuck to my hair.

****

Sticky tape stuck to the carpet,

Sticky tape stuck to the wall,

Sticky tape stuck to my trainers,

The curtains, the dog's special ball.

****

Sticky tape stuck to the table,

The plates and the mugs and my cup...

Anywhere else but the parcels -

No wonder they call me

STUCK UP !
****

THE CHRISTMAS - PRESENT WRAPPER.

****

I'm a Christmas-Present Wrapper -
I'm a Rapper who can Wrap !
So when the people see my skills
They stare and cheer and clap.

I can wrap a Rudolph Reindeer,
I can wrap a tiny box,
I can wrap a bouncy football,
Or a Unicorn that rocks.

I can battle with the sticky tape,
Or snip the sheet Just-So.
I can write a fancy label,
I can tie a shiny bow.

I'm all stuck up with glitter,
I've been wrapping night and day,
I sometimes think I might have gone
And wrapped my life away !

I'm a perfect Present-Wrapper,
(Though I know I shouldn't brag),
But as for all the gifts I'VE bought...
I'll bung them
In a BAG !

****

THE MUSIC OF CHRISTMAS.
****

(For Tricia and Chris.)

This is the Music our Christmas will make -
When Mum CLATTERS dishes
For mince pies and cakes.

Dad will untangle the lights on their string -
They'll shine for a moment,
Then blink and go PING.

The Cat will chase baubles, then jump in the box -
To YOWL at our Fairy
And tangle her socks.

Soon Gran will arrive with a cold in her head -
She'll snuffle and SNEEZE,
As her nose turns bright red.

A Choir on our doorstep will merrily sing -
Of a stable, a star,
And the SWISH of a wing.

Now everyone hopes that Old Santa will know -
We've TRIED to be good,
When he laughs: "HO ! HO ! HO !"

And just after midnight, a Sleighbell will JINGLE -
As stockings are filled
And the World starts to TINGLE.

Then early next morning, the Children will wake -
To a RUSTLE of paper
And presents to SHAKE...
AND

We'll ALL feel the love that makes wishes come true -
As we smile and we shout:
"HAPPY CHRISTMAS TO YOU !"

****

(Have fun with all those jolly Sound-Effects.)

OUR CRAZY LOCKDOWN CHRISTMAS.
****
Summer 2020.

Our lives were SO boring, we all heaved a sigh -
Then somebody said: "Let's give Christmas a try !"
For no special reason. We didn't ask why...

But the days were so dreary, our hopes hit the wall,
So we ransacked the loft, hung a star in the hall,
While Dad (wearing antlers) threw sweets at us all.

We dangled our garlands of holly leaves (fake);
There were cards to be crafted; a Grotto to make,
As Mum perched a penguin on top of a cake.

We couldn't find crackers to rattle and flap,
But we told silly jokes and we all shouted, 'SNAP !'
Then we sang happy songs so our Granny could clap.

The pot-plants wore tinfoil; the puppy wore wings;
We wrapped empty boxes with ribbons and strings,
As we acted a play about camels and kings.

We sat round a picture of flickery flames;
We tried to guess film-stars and world-famous names;
Then we all got the giggles - invented daft games...

When suddenly, somehow, without any snow
We all heard a jingle, a merry: "HO ! HO !"
We gazed at each other. The room seemed to glow -

Our house was still dusty. Our paintings still wet.
There weren't any glittering tables to set;
Or huge heaps of presents. Or riches -

And yet
That was the Christmas
We'll never forget."

****

CHEATING CHRISTMAS.
****

All my presents look like treats,
Flashy toys and games and treats...

Here's a large
And lumpy box -
Full of boring
Winter SOCKS.

Here's a Sporty
Car to race ?
No ! It's just
A PENCIL CASE.

Here's a parcel
Wrapped in tape...
Massive PANTS,
Wrong size. Wrong shape.

Here's a kit
Called 'Making Money'.
A PIGGY BANK -
Not filled. Not funny !

And here's the meanest
Gift of all,
Packaged like a
Basket Ball...
Rip the wrappings
Full of hope -
Out fall smelly
Bars of SOAP.

All my presents LOOK like treats -
Most of them are
Christmas
CHEATS.

****

(Let's hope this Stocking brings better luck !)

READY, STEADY...
****

Stand by your stockings,
Whistles blow -
Grab those presents,
Off you go !

Here's a book
Called 'Did You Know?';
Here's a ball
To catch and throw;
Here's a plastic
Buffalo ?
Here's a seed
To plant and grow;
Here's a thing
Which seems to glow;
Here's a kit to
Cut and sew;
Here's a tiny
Radio;
Here's a ticket
For a Show;
Here's a dome
That's full of Snow...
AND
Here's an orange
In the
TOE !

Who's the Winner ?
Don't you know ?
EVERYBODY !
Ho ! Ho ! Ho !

****

CHRISTMAS NIGHT.

****

The bedroom shelf
Is crammed with toys -
Most of them built
To make a noise.

Toys with levers
And toys with lights,
Computer games
For computer fights.

Robot armies
With whirling blades,
Plastic soldiers
For midnight raids.

Wind-up puppies
That bark and spin,
Mechanical dolls
With teeth that grin.

Gadgets that endlessly
Play a tune -
Brightly gleaming
Beneath the Moon.

But all the same
It's dear old Ted
With his one, loose ear
That I'll take to bed.

****

HOORAY FOR CHARLES DICKENS.

****

(He wrote 'A Christmas Carol' - and perhaps you have seen a
film of the story on T.V. I liked the 'Muppets' version best!)

Hooray for Charles Dickens !
The man to remember
When stories are told
In the dark of December.

The Weaver of Words
Who conjured a spell
And crafted a legend
To tell. And re-tell.

The tale of a Miser
With ice in his heart,
Whose greed and whose loneliness
Set him apart.

The Cratchits who owned
Neither rubies nor rings,
Yet, measured by kindness,
Were richer than Kings.

And merry old Fezziwig,
Warm as the Sun,
Who lit up his workplace
With feasting and fun -

While Scrooge, dragged from sleep
By the clock's hollow chime,
Was haunted by Spirits
And taunted by Time...

To show us that LOVE
Is more precious than gold -
A true Christmas message
That's told. And re-told.
SO
Hooray for Charles Dickens -
The Ghost from the Past,
Who gave us a Present
To share.
And to last.

****

WHAT WOULD WE DO WITHOUT CHRISTMAS ?

****

What would we do without Christmas ?
No shepherds, no manger, no hay ?
No angels with wings and a halo,
Dressed up for the end-of-term play ?

What would we do without Christmas ?
Where in the World would we be ?
Without any holly and ivy,
The fairy on top of the tree ?

What would we do without Christmas ?
Old Santa, the Grotto, the queue,
The Elves and the Gnomes in the work-shop,
The snow on the roof (stuck with glue) ?

What would we do without Christmas ?
The lights and the flickering flames ?
The presents, the crackers, the laughter,
The favourite, family games ?

What would we do without Christmas ?
The food that takes ages to bake ?
The cards with their robins and reindeer,
The snowmen who smile on the cake ?

What would we do without Christmas ?
The caring, the sharing, the fun ?
The Panto, the jokes and the carols ?
Our walks in the bright, winter sun.

What would we do without Christmas -
The season we all love the best ?
We say - the World would be sadder...
But Mum says
She'd just have a rest !

* *

(Don't worry - she loves it really !)

THE CHRISTMAS CONJUROR.
****

The Christmas Conjuror
Pulls back his starry sleeves
And laces his long, frosty fingers.
Then he blows softly
On his bare knuckle-bones,
Winks at a wide-eyed child
And SNAP !
From his pale palms
The snowflakes flutter and rise like birds
On the glittering air,
Or whirl around our heads in silent swarms.

Now he claps his hands
Once, twice,
And snatches a silver hair
From his own, cold beard.
Moonlight touches the taut thread
As he twists it, shapes it,
Shakes it like a ribbon of silk
Until strings of icicles
Decorate the roof, the fence, the pale twigs
Of the apple tree.

At last, he raises his wand
To shower us with magic.
Beneath our feet
The grass is a crystal pathway,
Every hedge wears a necklace of royal webs,
And the green pond is a mirror
To reflect our wonder.

But when we turn to thank him,
The Christmas Conjuror
Has faded away
Like the echo
Of quiet laughter.

****

CHRISTMAS CREATURES

POLAR BEAR POEM.
****

"I'm not a greedy creature,"
Said the gloomy Polar Bear.
"I don't want fancy fittings
For my private, winter lair.
I don't want fancy clothing,
Since I'm rather fond of fur.
I don't want fancy dinners -
Frozen food's what I prefer !"

"I'm not a fat and friendly bear
Who wants a pot of honey;
And I don't do any shopping,
So I don't want bags of money.
I don't want fancy footwear,
Since my paws are made of leather;
I don't want tubes of sun-screen
Since I don't have sunny weather."

"And I don't want fluffy duvets
Or a cosy rocking-chair -
So I'm NOT a greedy creature,"
Sighed the gloomy Polar Bear...
"But life is rather boring
In a land of ice and snow,
SO
I would be REALLY grateful if
Your sleigh could swoop quite low -
Then whizz me round the midnight sky...
With Rudolph,
OFF WE GO !"

****

PENGUIN PUZZLE.

****

There's a Penguin on our doorstep !
He says he wants to know
If we've seen a passing iceberg ?
Or an igloo ? Or some snow ?

He says he thinks he lost them
When a sea-fog sort of swirled,
So he went and missed his turning
For the Far-End Of The World.

He's MUCH too tired to waddle
To the Penguin Orphanage -
And he says he's feeling peckish...

Can we keep him in our fridge ?

****

PENGUIN PROBLEM.

****

Oh,
Pity the Penguin
Now Christmas is here -
His day is the same
As the rest of the year.

There isn't a tree
And there's nowhere to go
For parties and crackers...
Just snow.
And more snow.
And inside his stocking
There aren't many treats,
Just boring old fishes
And fish-flavoured sweets.

And the stocking itself
Is so terribly small
There isn't much room
For a book, or a ball,
Or a cuddly toy,
Or some nice, cosy slippers
(Which simply aren't made
To fit Penguin-shaped flippers).

So he sits on an iceberg
With frost on each leg,
And he longs for a cushion
(Instead of an egg),
And his sad, Penguin eye
Drips a sad Penguin tear...
OH
Pity the Penguin
Now Christmas is here.

****

108

RICH PICKINGS.
****

Only a sliver of turkey,
Only a crust of bread,
Only a broken biscuit,
With butter that's thinly spread.
Only a shaving of Cheddar,
Only a flake of fish,
Only a crumb of pudding
To flavour a Christmas wish.
Only a spoonful of trifle,
Only a crumpled hat...

Only a Royal Banquet
For one rather grateful
Rat.

****

SMALL WONDER.

****

One year, the Must-Have present was a charming Mini-Pig.
The advert said: "They're house-trained and they don't grow very big."
So we ordered one for Christmas. We didn't pay too much -
It came complete with bucket and a special, piggy hutch.

The little soul was nervous, so it shivered and it sneezed,
But we tucked it in Mum's stocking and we reckoned she'd be pleased.
Our guess was right. She loved its tail, its tiny wrinkled snout,
Its spots, its floppy ear-flaps and the way it skipped about.

She called her piglet 'Petal' and it learned to Sit and Stay !
And though it stained the bathroom floor, it stole her heart away.
It also stole the best armchair, the best view of the telly...
The best of everything in fact - while growing HUGE and smelly.

Right now, I feel it watching me with naughty, piggy eyes -
It's trained us all to Run and Fetch. Its meals are Super-Sized.
The Moral Is:
An Advert never offers wise advice,
So if you want a Mini-Pet
You're better off with
MICE !

****

110

THE ZOO CREATURES' CHRISTMAS.
****

When Santa reached the sleepy Zoo,
He knew exactly what to do.
He sorted through his sack and sleigh
And left some treats
For Christmas Day...

Ginger socks for the Desert Fox,
Colourful ties for the Butterflies.
Soft grey gloves for the Turtle Doves,
Furry bloomers for chilly Pumas.

Slinky frocks for the Lady Crocs,
Enormous shoes for the Kangaroos.
Wrinkly pants for the Elephants,
Royal dresses for proud Lionesses.

Velvet capes for the elegant Apes,
Small red hats for the Vampire Bats.
Stripy suits for the noisy Coots,
Petticoats for the Nanny Goats.

A swirly scarf for the old Giraffe,
Smart, black clothes for Rooks and Crows.
Top hats and tails for the snooty Snails,
Comfy slippers for Sea-Lion flippers...
AND
Warm pyjamas for dreamy Llamas.

SO
Did the creatures cheer and purr ?
And were they pleased ?
Of course they were !

THE ZOO KEEPER'S CHRISTMAS.
****

The Zoo Keeper wanted a party
So he asked all his friends to drop by.
He promised them plenty of presents
Plus slices of pudding and pie.

The first to arrive were the Cheetahs,
Then the Monkeys turned up in a cart.
The Hyenas arrived with the giggles - So that was a pretty good
start.
The Birds and the Beasts quickly gathered,
Then sat round the table to wait...
They couldn't begin without Tortoise - And of course, he was
half-an-hour late !

But at last, the whole Zoo was assembled
And the party began with a swing...
The Gibbons all climbed up the curtains - To shout for the games
to begin.
The Leopards played 'Spot-The-Lost-Slipper,
The Vultures were playing 'I-Spy';
The Sloths won the 'Musical Statues' - Though the Zoo Keeper
gave it a try.

At teatime, the room fell quite silent,
Apart for the odd crunch and slurp.
They were all on their Christmas behaviour - So everyone tried
not to burp !
When every scrap had been eaten
The animals stood up and cheered...
But alas !
All their 'Thank Yous' were wasted - For the Keeper had just
disappeared...

"Well, don't look at me," hissed the Python,
Who was licking some crumbs from his tie.

"Nor me !" snapped a Crocodile sadly - As he wiped a big tear
from his eye.
But just as a fight seemed to threaten,
And the Lemurs began to hurl fruit -
The Keeper arrived down the chimney - With a beard and a huge
scarlet suit.

For each of his guests there were presents
To keep when they all wandered home...
For the Grizzly Bears there was honey - For the Walrus, some
bubble-bath foam.
The Parrots were given a joke book;
Bags of hay for the wild mountain Horse;
There were bow-ties and gloves for the Penguins - For the
Zebras, pyjamas, of course !

At midnight, the party was over,
Since everything comes to an end...
So the animals left for their shelters - After saying: 'Good Night'
to their friend.
The Zoo Keeper stood on his doorstep,
Just waving for all he was worth -
Then went up to bed with his supper - The Happiest Keeper On
Earth.

****

THE FOXY RIDER.

****

An Almost True Story !

There's a Fox on our bus -
And he's seeing the sights !
He's gazing in wonder
At dazzling lights...

Or glittering trees,
Or a reindeer's red nose,
Or great, golden stars,
Or a penguin that glows...

Or camels, or angels,
Or mangers with hay,
Or a whiskery man
Who is rocking a sleigh...

Our Fox sees the children
With Christmassy smiles,
He watches the shoppers
For long, bouncy miles...

Until he's released
In his own, homely wood -
Where he warns little foxcubs
To try to be GOOD !

Then, maybe at midnight,
When frosty leaves CRUNCH...
Their own Santa Claws
Will bring tit-bits to munch,
Plus magical treats
For their first
Christmas Lunch !

****

This fox really did climb to the top of a bus in London - and sat on the front seat !
The passengers called the R.S.P.C.A. -
and Foxy was released into the woodland where his journey began.
BUT
I'm not really sure what he told his family !

****

SANTA'S CAT.
****

Santa's Cat, like all her kind,
Is known to chop and change her mind...

When every door is firmly shut,
She'll wake and stretch and mew and strut
Across the Grotto's frosty floor,
To scrabble at the kitchen door.
And THEN, when Santa sets her free,
She'll scamper back demanding tea !

But only THIS and only THAT,
(She is a most annoying cat)
And lazy too, since Lands of Ice
Are rarely over-run by mice !

So,
Why does Santa keep this pest...
Who leaves her fluff on knee and vest,
Who pulls great holes in scarlet suits,
Who hides her toys inside his boots,
Who makes a tangle of his beard,
And is (by nervous Penguins) feared ?

Well,
When Old Santa's feeling fraught,
And not as jolly as he ought,
(Because his mind is in a whirr)
He likes to hear her friendly purr,
And when the winter blizzard blows
It's Santa's Cat
Who warms his toes !

****

NOT JUST FOR CHRISTMAS.
****

Santa's Dog will never win
A shiny cup at Crufts -
He can't remember tricks he's taught,
His coat sticks out in tufts.

The Snowmen found him freezing -
A scruffy, midnight stray.
But the Reindeer soon revived him
With a heap of steaming hay.

So now, he chases Penguins,
He barks at Polar Bears,
He chews a stolen bobble hat
(The sort that Santa wears).

The Gnomes say he's a nuisance
With his naughtiness and noise,
But still - they scratch his tummy
While he dribbles on the toys.

He scampers after Rudolph,
He tries to fly, I'm told,
While Santa says he's far too SLOW
To catch a Winter Cold !

But when the sleigh goes sailing -
His Dog sits in the back -
And though he couldn't scare a moth,
He THINKS he guards the sack.

That's why he shares the fireside
With Santa's jolly Wife,
And Santa -
And the Grotto Cat,
For Christmas...And for Life.

****

(In our world, Polar Bears and Penguins live
at opposite ends of the Earth -
but Santa-World is magical - so anything can happen !)

THE LONELY TEDDY BEAR.
****

The walls of the Toy Shop were shining
With glitter and stars painted gold,
Each doll and each game,
Each puzzle and train
Had either been ordered or sold.

But there, in a heap by the window,
Where a 'Bargain' sign drooped like a tear,
Sat a Teddy so tattered
So ancient and battered
That nobody ever came near.

Its growl was a rather sad hiccup,
Or sometimes a pitiful cough;
Its fur, worn and frayed
Had started to fade
And one of its eyes had come off.

"I'll never sell this," groaned the Owner,
As Christmas Eve came to a close.
"If it's here at New Year,
Then it's out on its ear.."
And he smacked it quite hard on its nose !

The doors were all bolted and shuttered,
The shop-girls had giggled and gone,
The tree, once so bright,
Had been dimmed for the night...
And only the Bear lingered on.

"I'll never have someone to love me,
I'll never have someone to hug,
I'll be left on the shelf
All alone, by myself,"
Said the Bear with a brave little shrug.

But far away, over the city,
A sleigh glided by like a dream,
With just a faint jingle
To give you a tingle
As lamps lit the sky with a gleam.

Old Santa was weary of chimneys,
He'd given out toys by the ton,
He was just about ready
To post his last Teddy
When he noticed a short-fall of ONE !

His cherry red cheeks turned quite sickly,
He gulped as he searched through his sack...
But all that he found
Was a hole, big and round
And he didn't have time to turn back

He pulled out a note from his pocket,
It came from a street cold and bleak...
Each word that he read
Made him shake his tired head,
And he felt too embarrassed to speak.

'Dear Santa,' it said. "I'm an orphan.
I don't get much money to spend,
But I hope you can spare
One small Teddy Bear,
To love me and be my best friend.'

At once, he was bribing the Reindeer
With carrots and bags of mince pies,
To hunt through the town
For a Bear golden-brown,
To give as a special surprise...
So Rudolph and Partners went speeding
Past High Street and market and shop,
Till they spied a weak glow
From a window below -
And they skidded their hoofs to a stop.

Our Teddy gazed up full of wonder
As Santa appeared at his side -
And somehow, he knew
That his wish had come true
When he sailed on that magical ride.

In the moonlight his ears softly glistened,
In the starlight his furry coat gleamed,
As hands good and kind
Touched the patch that was blind
And a new button-eye proudly beamed.

Next morning, a child laughed with pleasure
And lovingly stroked the Bear's face -
While the man from the store
Found the Teddy no more !
Just a small pile of soot in its place.

****

SANTA TO THE RESCUE.
****

Old Santa is a kindly soul,
So when his deer retire -
He nips off to the Rescue Home
To see what he can hire.

This year - he hit a problem.
The woman shook her head,
"No reindeer, Sir. I'm sorry -
Would a rabbit do instead ?
Or what about a gerbil ?
Or a rather charming hen ?
(She's not a distance-flier,
But she flutters now and then)."

Santa did his best to hide
The panic in his eyes:
"I need a creature swift enough
To cross the Christmas skies.
I need a pet that's strong enough
To drag a sleigh," he said...
And at that anxious moment
Something grunted in the shed.

"That's Lulu," groaned the woman,
"She smells a little bit -
And she's rather plump and grubby,
But she's frisky. And she's fit."
So Santa paid the Rescue Fee
(Which wasn't very big)
Then introduced his reindeer
To their team-mate - Lulu Pig !

So - if you hear at midnight
Farmyard noises in the sky,
Or if you catch the pitter-pat
Of trotters trotting by...
Remember - Santa's MAGIC,
And at Christmas
PIGS CAN FLY !

****

REINDEER RAP.

****

We're a fly-high team,
We're a hot-hoof band,
With our jingle bells
From a magic land.
When we pull that sleigh,
When we go, man, go,
When we bring F.C.
With his: "Ho ! Ho ! HO !"
When we get on down
To your sleepy street,
When we rock your roof
To a hip-hop beat,
When we stomp away
Through the starry sky,
You can make a wish
As we boogy by.
You can shake your hands,
You can stamp your toe,
You can strut your stuff
In the cool Yule snow,
You can shout and cheer,
Set the whole world clapping -
We're the Reindeer Band
And
We're Christmas Rapping !

****

REINDEER SCHOOL.

****

At Reindeer School - Beginners learn:
How to start.
And stop. And turn.
How to fly with home-made wings
(Till they get the hang of things).
How to jingle (not too soon)
How to skim across the Moon.

How to dodge the Space-Race junk,
How to land without a CLUNK !
How to soar above a plane,
Then to plummet DOWN again.

How to race with bird and bat...
Plus a Snowman. Fancy that !
How to zoom as fast as light,
Round the World in just one night.

How to follow (when it snows)
Dear old Rudolph's shiny nose.
How to find each road and street -
Sat-Nav simply can't compete.

How to balance on a roof.
How to skate on just one hoof.
How to munch mince pies at night,
Also carrots (while in flight).

Then, when Santa's work is done,
Whoosh back home and beat the Sun.
That's what Reindeer need to know -

Just ask Santa..."Ho, ho, ho !"

********************

WHAT SHALL WE DO WITH THE
RED-NOSED REINDEER ?

****

(To the tune of: 'What Shall We Do With The Naughty Sailor.')

Verse One:
What shall we do with the Red-Nosed Reindeer,
What shall we do with the Red-Nosed Reindeer,
What shall we do with the Red Nosed Reindeer,
On our Christmas morning ?

Verse Two:
Pop him in a stocking to amaze Aunt Mary,
Fix him on a fir tree with a festive Fairy,
Send him with a present to our local Dairy,
When the day is dawning.

Chorus:
Hooray ! We like surprises - Hooray ! We like surprises.
Hooray ! We like surprises - On our Christmas morning.

Repeat Verse One.

Verse Three:
Tickle him with tinsel till we drive him crazy,
Let him play with puzzles till his eyes go hazy,
Teach him how to Tango with a Cow called Daisy,
When our dinner's warming.

Repeat The Chorus and Verse One.

Verse Four:
Dress him up in slippers and a silly sweater,
Take him to the Panto when he's looking better,
Send him back to Santa with a 'Thank You' letter,
When we all start yawning.

Final Chorus:

That's what we did with the Red-Nosed Reindeer,
That's what we sang with the Red-Nosed Reindeer,
THAT'S why he WANTS to visit US again dear,
On our Christmas Morning.

****

'TIS THE SEASON FOR A SELFIE.
****

(Spoken by Santa !)

"Oh look ! Rudolph's sent me a Selfie.
There he is, peeping over his door.
He wants me to say that I 'LIKE HIM',
Though I've told him quite often before...

In fact, he's sent DOZENS of Selfies,
To the Gnomes and the Penguins and Me -
Rudolph in front of the Grotto;
Rudolph on top of the tree;
Rudolph with Frosty the Snowman;
Or munching a massive mince pie;
Or dressed in the Fairy's pink tu-tu,
Or zooming around in the sky.

Rudolph in HUNDREDS of poses,
Yet still he keeps sending me more !
Rudolph in so many places
He's quickly becoming a bore.
Good grief ! He's just sent me another,
Though it's late and I'm tucked up in bed...
Rudolph dressed up as a Robot
With an aerial stuck on his head.

I've seen him with Soap Stars and Heroes,
At Someone's Celebrity Ball -
Sometimes I catch myself hoping
He'll slip on a carrot and fall.
I've tried to be terribly patient,
But when will this Selfie Stuff end ?
If he pulls any more funny faces
I'll finally go round the bend.

Oh no ! Here's a photo of Rudolph
In tights," Santa says with a groan.
"If he sends any more - I'll be SELF-ISH
And I'll just have to STAMP
On his phone !"

****

RUDOLPH'S 2020 GRUMBLE.

****

(He's grumpy because his red-nose can't glow when he wears a mask !)

Rudolph's in a dreadful mood,
He's off his friends, he's off his food -
He spends his day
Just kicking hay !
His language (frankly) can be RUDE.

The other Reindeer whizz - and wear
Their masks without a single care.
In fact, they're warm
In snow and storm,
As well as beating germs. So there !

At last, Old Santa went to see
Why Rudolph ranted: "Look at me !
This ghastly thing
Tied on with string
Has stolen my identity."

"My life is wrecked. I've lost my pride.
I'm ruined," Rudolph sniffed and sighed.
"My nose can't glow
Can't guide you, so -
I'm USELESS now," the poor Deer cried.

BUT
Santa (with his Elves and Co.)
Said: "Cheer up Rudolph. Off we go !
You'll lead my sleigh
Your bright, light way...
We don't need masks outdoors, you know."

While Snowmen yelled:
"WE TOLD YOU SO !"

****

(Thank goodness Rudolph's nose is glowing again.)

A JINGLY-JANGLY, FLIPPY-FLAPPY, RED-NOSED REQUEST !

****

You've guessed it ! I'm Rudolph -
The Nose was a Clue !
I fly through the sky
To bring presents for YOU.

I jingle my bells
At the front of the sleigh,
And I NEVER complain -
Though I'm sick of cold hay.

I soar over rooftops
In frost and in snow,
Then land in a flurry
With nostrils aglow.

I wait while Old Santa
Slides down to your room,
He seems to take ages,
Then UP with a zoom -

He's sooty but happy !
He's found tasty treats -
Chocolate cakes
And his favourite sweets...

My mouth starts to water !
My hopes RISE - then FALL.
I'm given a vegetable
Mucky and small.

SO

If you are planning
My Christmas surprise -
Don't leave me a carrot...
Just yummy mince pies.

****

THE REINDEER COUNTDOWN.
****

TEN flying Reindeer - Swooping in a line,
One hit an asteroid !
So then there were NINE.

NINE flying Reindeer - Leaving slightly late,
One got a speeding fine -
So then there were EIGHT.

EIGHT flying Reindeer - Racing over Devon,
One stopped for tea and scones -
So then there were SEVEN.

SEVEN flying Reindeer - Crashing into bricks !
One went to Casualty...
So then there were SIX.

SIX flying Reindeer - Practising a dive,
One snapped an antler,
So then there were FIVE.

FIVE flying Reindeer - Splashing by the shore,
One tried to ride a shark,
So then there were FOUR.

FOUR flying Reindeer - Skimming past a tree,
One annoyed the Fairy,
So then there were THREE.

THREE flying Reindeer - Visiting the Zoo,
One teased the Crocodile,
So then there were TWO.

TWO flying Reindeer - Circling the Sun,
One burned his shiny nose,
So then there was ONE.

ONE flying Reindeer - Having Christmas fun -
He burst a BIG balloon,
So then there were NONE.

(NO flying Reindeer ? Please don't shed a tear -
Santa kindly told me,
They'll ALL be back
Next Year.)

****

CHRISTMAS CHARACTERS

SNOWMAN SCHOOL.
****

In a Frosty Land - By a frosty pool...
What do Snowmen learn at school ?

How to grow quite fast. And fat !
How to wear a bobble hat.
How to stand in just ONE place
With a carrot on your face.

How to wave your twiggy hands
When a friendly Robin lands.
How to guard the garden gate,
How to daydream while you wait.

How to smile all day. And night !
How to give the fox a fright.
Later, when the shadows creep,
When your humans are asleep...

How to float above the ground,
Flap your scarf and fly around !
How to sing an icy tune
As you circle past the moon.

How to watch with wonky eyes,
Reindeer skimming through the skies.
How to scare the Big Bad Cat
When you land beside him - SPLAT !

Than, one warm and sunny day,
How to melt and drift away...
How to leave without one tear -
Knowing you'll be back. Next year.
SO

That's what Snowmen learn at school -
How to be completely
COOL !
****

ONLY A SNOWMAN.
****

Only a Snowman
Glistening, fat,
Scarf made from tinsel,
Crumpled old hat.

Only a Snowman
Nobody loves,
Bottle-top buttons,
Moth-eaten gloves.

Only a Snowman
Standing outside,
Battered by blizzards,
Losing my pride.

Only a Snowman
Watching the skies,
Staring at shadows
With small, stony eyes.

Only a Snowman
Not built to run,
Dreading the dawn
Of the warm, winter Sun.

Only a Snowman
Turning to slush,
Watching my body
Melt in a rush.

Only a Snowman,
Friend for a day,
Softly and secretly
Slipping away.

Only a puddle,
And one carrot nose -
But maybe you'll find me
The next time it
SNOWS.

****

SNOW MYSTERY.

****

(This poem is called a Mono-Rhyme.)

Nobody knew and nobody knows
Who ran away with our Snowman's nose !

Was it a Squirrel on swift, grey toes ?
An army of Fieldmice in marching rows ?

A Rabbit who woke from her winter doze ?
A Dragon from woods where the Flame Tree grows ?

A Witch with a wand that wickedly glows ?
A feathery Horse ? Or a nestful of Crows ?

Nobody knew and nobody knows,
Because, in a dazzle, the Sun arose -

To smile in the sky - as our friend unfroze
And flew to a Land where the Dream-Wind blows.

So, let us all wish, and let us suppose
He's home again, happily
Wearing his nose.

****

(One year, someone sent Clare a Christmas Card,
with a picture of a Donkey munching a carrot !
Perhaps that's the answer ?
Or do YOU have a better idea ?)

139

SNOW JOKE !

****

Why does it have to be Snowmen ?
Why is it NEVER Snowgirls ?
Why can't we build a Snow-Princess
With berries for rubies and pearls ?

Why can't we pick her some holly
To give her a spiky green crown ?
What about icicle diamonds
To wear on her glittering gown ?

What about crowds of Snow-Ladies
With twiggy and twizzly hair ?
They could stand on our lawn looking grumpy
With placards that say:
'IT'S NOT FAIR !'

Then...

We'll give them a huge heap of snowballs
To throw at the Snowmen for fun -
And maybe, when everyone's laughing,
Our Snowgirls will chorus:

"WE'VE WON !"

****

(Here are a few, frosty ideas - if there isn't much snow !

SNOW DOG.
****

Our Snow-Dog is quiet and small,
But he's frightened of NOTHING at all,
With his cabbage-leaf ears
And his teeth sharp as spears,
He's faithfully guarding our wall.

In dawnlight and starlight he's here,
So we know we have nothing to fear...
But if he should stray
One warm, winter's day,
We'll find him - when snow falls
Next year.

****

SNOW CAT.
****

I've built a cuddly Snow-Cat
With whiskers made from straws -
And I'm almost sure,
I'm ALMOST sure
I saw him lick his paws.

He's sitting in my garden,
He's smiling at me now -
And I'm almost sure,
I'm ALMOST sure
I heard him say: "Mee-ow !"

****

141

SNOW-PET.
****

This year, we didn't have much snow,
We couldn't build a Man - and so
We made a little Mouse to show.

His whiskers twitch when cold winds blow,
His nose (a berry) seems to glow,
His stringy tail flicks to and fro !

He isn't scared of Cat or Crow,
And though he's rather shy, you know,
I'm sure I heard him squeak:
"Hello !"

****

STRICTLY COME DANCING ON ICE.

****

Four famous Snowmen grace the ice -
It's nice to see them circle twice,
Around the rink on speedy feet,
All keen and eager to compete...

But now it's time for Number Five -
He's wrecking Rumba, Waltz and Jive,
He's spoiling Sambas, squashing toes -
And how he stays here - no one knows !

The frosty Judges mutter madly -
"He's only good at skating BADLY !"
"He's old. He's clumsy. He's a clown."
"Let's vote him out. Or melt him down !"

At this - a Snowgirl, pale yet proud,
Comes twirling by, to tell the crowd:
"These experts are a stupid lot !
Ignore the scores. They've lost the plot...

My partner may not glide with style
Or gusto - but he makes me SMILE."
And as the Band begins to play
The grumpy Judges slink away...

While ALL the Snowmen dance till dawn,
Till Reindeer snore and Fairies yawn -
And NO ONE asks: "Who's lost ? Who's won ?"
Since no one cares -
They've just had FUN.

****

TEN GRUMPY SNOWMEN.
****
(A Count-Down Poem For Ten Readers - In Bobble Hats and Scarves.)

TEN grumpy Snowmen - Standing in a line.
One joined the Grotto Queue - So then there were NINE.

NINE grizzly Snowmen - Tired and cross and late.
One missed his Bus Ride home - So then they were EIGHT.

EIGHT grouchy Snowmen - Driving down to Devon.
One stuck in mud and flood - So then there were SEVEN.

SEVEN sniffy Snowmen - Hunting for some sticks.
One broke a twiggy hand - So then there were SIX.

SIX huffy Snowmen - Wishing they could dive.
One tumbled in the pond - So then there were FIVE.

FIVE ratty Snowmen - Grumbled more and more.
One grew hot and steamy - So then there were FOUR.

FOUR moody Snowmen - Chopping down a tree.
One snapped his carrot-nose - So then there were THREE.

THREE gloomy Snowmen - Sounding sad and blue.
One lost his happy smile - So then there were TWO.

TWO silly Snowmen - Smiling at the Sun.
One (like magic) disappeared - So then there was ONE.

ONE lonely Snowman - Went and wished for rain !
Splashed in all the puddles - Then dribbled down the drain...

NO grumpy Snowmen - To drip an icy tear...
Bring them back on Boxing Day
And start again
NEXT YEAR.
****

SANTA'S LITTLE HELPER.
****

The tiniest Elf - on his dusty old shelf
Was lonely, unloved and forgotten.
He wished he could pack -
Santa's sleigh. Or his sack,
But he knew that his prospects were rotten.

He didn't have muscles - to tackle the tussles
With parcels that jam in the door.
And as for his height,
Well, it might be all right
If stockings were hung on the floor !

But one year (I'm told) - as he shivered with cold,
A Christmas Tree Fairy flapped by.
Her wand wasn't new,
It was mended with glue,
But she waved it and gave it a try.

The Elf heard a PING ! - And the swish of a wing,
As Santa slumped down in a chair.
With a groan and a sigh
He seemed ready to cry !
"It's time for my ride through the air ?"

"I need someone small - who can find things that fall
Into places where Snowmen can't squeeze.
The Penguins have tried
But their feet are too wide,
And the Bears bang their elbows and knees."

The Elf, with a yelp - cried: "Please let me help !"
And Santa replied: "Right away...
Tonight's Christmas Eve
And would you believe ?
I've just dropped the key for my sleigh !"

So our Elf swiftly dangled - where cobwebs were tangled,
In places where treasures can hide...
And there, in a gap - As tight as a trap
He rescued the key. And his pride.

Well, the Elf won a prize - a trip round the skies,
Plus a Dolls' House to live in. Hooray !
Now nobody sneers
At his size. Or his ears...
He's the Helper who saved Christmas Day !

****

THE IGLOO BLUES.
****

I'm a HUGE hungry Elf -
And my chocolate money
Was spent on my rent
So my life isn't funny.

I am out in the cold
Which is not very nice -
My nose has gone red
And it's dripping with ice.

I've stayed near the Grotto
For long, frosty ages,
Wishing for work
And a big bag of wages.

I wish I could welcome
A Christmassy queue,
And choose jolly presents
For children like you.

I'd always be cheerful
And warm by the fire,
With the Penguins, the Fairy,
The Snow-Ladies' Choir...

But instead, I just shiver
And try not to sniff,
Though my raggy, green jumper
Is frozen and stiff.

Now my toes have gone numb
In my old, pointy shoes,
So here I am - singing
My sad Winter Blues.

A GIANT-SIZED ELF
Isn't wanted today....
But wait !
I've been hired
To help Santa - Hooray !

He's paid me a FORTUNE
To push-start his Sleigh.

THE ELF - AND - SAFETY RAP.
****

We're a mean, green team -
We're the Safety Elves -
We will take the glitter - from your Toy Shop shelves.

We will grab the glue,
Which is no surprise;
We will ban the Bears - with their beady eyes.

We will scrap the kits
With the tiny parts;
We will snatch your sword - and your pointy darts.

We will pulp the paints
That could make you sick;
We will crush the cars - that you just might lick.

We will swipe the swings
And your slippy slide;
We will smash that Dolly - with the spikes inside !

We will steal your sweets
And before we fly,
We will shake our heads - when you start to cry.

We will read the Rules,
We will wreck your day,
Then we'll bash your gadgets - and we'll run away.

We're the Safety Elves
And our work's begun...
We're a Mean, Green Team
And we're having
FUN !

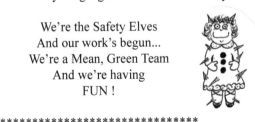

****
What a rotten lot - BOO !

149

THE ELF AND THE SNOWMAN.

****

The Elf and the Snowman
Who stood on the cake,
Are back in their tin
With a rattle and shake.

And there they will stay
For a dark, dreary year -
The Elf has a holly leaf
Jammed in his ear.

The Snowman (with icing
Still glued to his base)
Has a small, plastic Penguin
Pecking his face.

Yet the Elf and the Snowman
Still smile and still dream
Of magical tea-times,
With jokes - and ice-cream !

And children who giggle,
As crackers appear,
While the Elf and Snowman
Come back - Every year...

To stand on their snowy
And sugar-white floor -
So they're counting the days
Till it's Christmas
Once more !

****

THE FAIRY IN THE LOFT.
****

In a box that's gone soft,
I've been left in the loft,
So sometimes I think I'm forgotten -
But the Moths in my sock
Have embroidered my frock,
With delicate holes in the cotton.

My wings have come loose
(They were never much use)
But the Bat says they're fine as they are -
And the Spiders are fond
Of my droopy old wand -
They can bungee-jump right off my star.

In my small, silver shoes
The mice like to snooze -
They're smelly, but eager to please,
And if I feel sad,
Life isn't so bad
When they squeak happy songs to my knees.

My tinsel was knotted
Until a Rat spotted
The problem and gave it a chew.
And when I'm afraid
That my magic might fade -
He whispers: "Your dreams will come true."

That's when I remember
My first, fine December -
The glitter - the gifts far below.
But I love my new friends
So, if Santa Claus sends
A treat just for me - I will GLOW !

Now my lid lightly raises,
A bulb brightly blazes !
"Here she is !" someone laughs. "She's so sweet -
With some sparkle and glue,
Plus a sticker or two,
She'll soon make our Christmas complete."

Now I'm free ! Look at me,
At the top of my tree
Shiny new, with the World at my feet.
And when Christmas is done
I'll have plenty of fun -
With my friends in the loft.
What a treat !

****

THE WINTER - WORLD WORKERS.
****

I wonder how Santa
And all his good friends
Fill up their time, when their Winter-Work ends ?

Well...
The Fairy's a Circus-Star,
Hitting the heights,
On a flying trapeze
In her shiny, pink tights.

Rudolph's a Postman
Who hoofs down your street,
To jingle your bell
And deliver a treat.

The Gnomes from the Work-Shop
Repair broken toys -
Fixing the problems
For small girls and boys.

The Snowmen make mountains
Of ice-cream all day,
Then snooze in the fridge
So they won't melt away.

The Penguins are Waiters -
They're smart and they're willing.
They waddle at speed...
While their soup-bowls start spilling !

The Elves like to grumble -
They're eager and keen
To save all our trees...
And to shout: "Let's Go Green !"

153

And as for Old Santa -
It's no big surprise...
He's the Number One Taster
Of Merry Mince-Pies !

So
Santa and Company
Don't need a rest...
They're doing the jobs that they all LOVE the best.

****

Santa's
Pie Shop.

NAME THAT SLEIGH.
****

Old Santa launched a contest
(In his cool and sparky way)
He asked the Winter World to choose
A name he could display
In red (or maybe silver)
On his famous, magic sleigh.

At once, a foolish Penguin
With a waddle and a towel,
Suggested: 'Sleigh-McSleigh-Face' -
But the Bears began to growl !
They wanted: 'Festive Flier',
Which was 'liked' by Snowy Owl.

The Fairies waved their winter-wands
And wished for 'Shooting Star'.
The Wolf-Cubs fancied 'Sacks Away !'
The Snowmen flew quite far
To offer: 'Rocket Racer'.
While an Elf yelled: 'Christmas Car'.

The Gnomes liked 'Jolly Jingles'
And the Reindeer shouted, "Please !
We want 'The Rudolph Rover'
Or: 'The Supersonic Sneeze'."
Till poor Old Santa cried: "Enough !
My brain's begun to freeze."

He sorted through the mighty list
Beside the fire - and fretted,
As Mrs. Santa mopped his brow
With snowballs (while he sweated).
Until, at last, he chose the words
That wouldn't be regretted.
BUT

Whatever had he chosen ?
And WHO had won the prize ?
Away he sailed inside his sleigh,
Its name flashed round the skies !
He'd called it: Santa's Space-Ship'
Which had come as NO surprise...

That's the one he wrote HIMSELF -
So he won ALL the Pies !

****

Santa's Space-Ship

PANTOMIME TIME.
****

CHORUS:
At last it's joke and laughter time,
It's happy-ever-after time -
For hearing tales in song and rhyme,
With people from the Pantomime.

THE WICKED WITCH.
Don't BOO ! Or call me nasty - I'm really kind and good...
I'll prove it if you step inside - my cottage in the wood.
So when I offer lollipops - or gingerbread that's hot,
And tell you I'm a sweetie,
Don't shout: "Oh No You're Not !"

UGLY SISTERS.
We're beautiful ! We're charming ! - The Prince is sure to see,
He's found his future Princess - while Cinders cooks our tea.
I know you think we're nasty - and as bad as rotten eggs,
But we didn't ask for massive feet
To dangle from our legs !

DICK WHITTINGTON.
Dick Whittington they call me - I trudged to London Town.
They said the streets were made of gold - but stories let me down.
I sing. I dance. I hear Bow Bells - I wear a fancy hat...
But all the children want to see
Is Tom - my stupid CAT !

CAPTAIN HOOK.
You must remember Captain Hook - who led the Pirate Band
And bravely fought with Peter Pan - in Never-Never Land.
But still, I'm always terrified - the Crocodile will find me -
So every time I walk on stage,
I have to: "LOOK BEHIND ME !"

DAISY THE COW.
I'm everybody's favourite - because I raise a laugh...
I'm at the front and followed by - My bouncy UDDER half !
You like it when I'm waltzing - and my bucket slowly spins,
But most of all you love it when
My milk comes out in TINS !

FINAL CHORUS.
So hip-hooray for laughter time,
With people from the
PANTOMIME !

****

CINDY - RELLER.
****

Cindy-Reller read the News -
'Royal Disco. Rock and Blues !'
Knew her clothes
Were far too scruffy,
(Cleaning jobs don't pay e-nuffy).

Boris Buttons (kind but poor)
Helped her brush the Cafe floor.
"Cheer up, Cindy. There's a chance
You may still go
To the dance...
My last pound could set you free,
IF
You try the Lottery !"

On the T.V. screen that night
Cindy's numbers sparkled bright.
Up she jumped
From battered chair:
"I've become a MILLIONAIRE !"

She sold her story to the Press,
She bought a cool designer dress,
Then crossed the town
To meet her Prince,
Wearing shoes that made her WINCE !

She kicked the glassy things away,
Danced barefoot till break of day -
While the Prince
Turned up his nose
At the sight of Cindy's toes...

Chose instead an Ugly Sister,
(A girl prepared
To risk a blister) !
Meanwhile, Cindy didn't care -
She bought the Cafe in the Square...

Then changed its name to:
'DREAMS COME TRUE'
And
Married Buttons.
QUITE RIGHT TOO.

****

SANTA'S STORYLAND SACK.
****

The Storyland Characters wrote out their lists,
Hoping that no one
Would ever be missed.

Now, Humpty Dumpty wanted
A proper parachute;
The Woman in a crowded Shoe
Was hoping for a Boot.

Mary-Mary longed to grow
A Beanstalk for herself;
While Mother Hubbard's little dog
Barked: "Food ! On every shelf."

Miss Muffet wanted one small bowl
Without a Spider in it;
Then Incy-Wincy softly asked
For Sunshine - every minute.

The King of Hearts, he licked his lips
And asked for Chocolate Money;
The Bears and Naughty Goldilocks
Demanded pots of Honey.

The Three Blind Mice were hoping for
Some lovely, stick-on Tails...
(The sort of Happy Ending
That is never found in Sales.)

Those Christmas Lists went on..and...on...
Some short. Some weighed a ton.
Thank goodness Santa's MAGIC - so he had a lot of fun:
He granted every jolly wish -
Well,
All except for one.

And THAT came from the Wicked Witch
Who said she needed Spells -
The nasty ones that make you cry
And leave disgusting smells.

So wise Old Santa left a book
Entitled: 'How To Be
A Sweet And Kindly Person.'
Then he signed it:
'Love From Me.'

THE CHRISTMAS GROTTO GAMES.
****
(Spoken by an excited but breathless Sports Reporter.)

And...
They're all lining up for the Grand Final -
Santa is testing his new spiky boots,
(Plain black as usual - ideal for sooty chimneys).
The Gnomes are still puffing
After a training run with the Polar Bear;
The Snowmen are adjusting their noses
(No wobbly carrots allowed)
And the Safety Elves are searching the Reindeer
For Go-Faster Spells.
Meanwhile, the Penguins are warming-up
With a spot of Egg-Juggling.
Rudolph is flashing his nose (which CAN'T be legal),
And the Grotto Elf, wearing soggy green slippers.
Doesn't have a hope !

The last few contestants are arriving just in time.
The Fairy's at the top of her twinkly tree,
She's waving her wand - and they're OFF...

The Penguins have fallen at the first fence,
The Chief Snowman has tripped over his own scarf,
And the Elf, as expected, has limped back to bed.
But the Gnomes, running in relays,
Have whizzed round the Igloo
And overtaken Prancer and Dancer
(Who probably ate too many mince pies).
Now, here comes the Polar Bear, looking dangerous -
He's already crossed the Glacier in record time
And he's just behind Rudolph
Who is simply flying along.
It's neck and antler,
Only Old Santa can beat them now...

They've reached the last obstacle
(A rather tempting stocking entirely filled with sweets).
The Gnomes can't resist,
Rudolph and Santa are sharing the toffees
And the Bear is chewing a chocolate mouse...
But wait !
Who is this, clopping past the pack and clanging her bell ?
Is it ? Can it be ?
YES ! It's Daisy the Pantomime Cow,
Winning Santa's Sack of Super Surprises -
And that, my friends, is what I call
An Udderly Happy Ending.

****

CHRISTMAS WITH SANTA

CHIMNEY POT PROBLEM.

****

How do you climb down a chimney
When a chimney-pot just isn't there ?
Do you poke toys through the cat-flap
And give poor old Fluffy a scare ?

Do you push parcels down drainpipes ?
Do you stuff gifts in the shed ?
Do you stick stamps on the wrappers
And post all the presents instead ?

Do you bring hammers and spanners
To burgle the bedrooms with force ?
Or simply fly home in a temper
And grumble until you grow hoarse ?

Dear Santa,
Please tell me the answer...

"I do it by MAGIC - of course !"

****

A BOOTIFUL CHRISTMAS.
****

One winter, when it drizzled for dreary days and weeks,
Santa found his wellie-boots
Were full of holes and leaks.
"You'll have to buy some new ones," his Wife said, firm yet kind.
So off they trudged through sleet and slush
To see what they could find.

Well, all the shoe-shops shimmered with wellies wild and weird,
But Santa's socks were soggy,
So he faced the deed he feared.
He opened up his wallet. He told the girl his size,
Then heard a long and jolly list
With panic in his eyes...

"Would Sir like these, with tassels ? Or yellow ones with flowers?
Or shiny stars and comets
With lights that blink for hours ?
Or extra posh and purple ones ? (A pair to wear with pride.)
Or else a Doctor Who design -
With LOTS of room inside ?

Or zebra stripes ? Or leopard spots ? Or grey, with rhino-wrinkles?
Or green, with funny, froggy eyes ?
Or these ? The cow-bell tinkles !"
Poor Santa felt all flustered. He stared at reds and blues...
He sighed and groaned and shuddered -
Till his Wife said: "Let ME choose."

That's why, on Christmas Morning, when you pull your curtains
back,
(And you happen to be lucky)
You'll spot Santa with his sack,
His hood, his sleigh, his reindeer
And his BOOTS - You've guessed -
They're BLACK.

****

MOTHER CHRISTMAS.
****

We all know that Santa is magic -
(Which is how he gets into our homes).
We all know he fills up our stockings,
With toys from the Toy-Making Gnomes.

We know that he keeps teams of reindeer,
And rides round the World on his sleigh;
We know that he wears a red jacket
And lives in a land far away...

BUT

What about old Mother Christmas ?
We don't know a thing about HER !
Like - does she wear big jolly jumpers ?
And does she cook puddings all year ?

Does she go shopping for carrots
And pies for the Christmas Eve crew ?
Does she read ALL the long letters
From small, hopeful children like you ?

And are her cheeks rosy as berries ?
And are her eyes sparky and bright ?
And does she like wrapping the presents ?
And does she sing Carols all night ?

And does she knit hats for the Snowmen ?
And does she hang cards on the door ?
And does she make Santa wear slippers
When sooty old boots smudge the floor ?

And does she like skating with Penguins ?
And does she love crackers ? And snow ?
And does she make everyone happy ?

I bet that your Mother will know.

****

THE YEAR FATHER CHRISTMAS WAS ILL.

****

"Oh no !" muttered Santa. "What can I do ?
I can't give the children this horrible flu' !"

"But who can I send on the Christmas Eve round ?
It has to be someone who won't make a sound.
Someone who's jolly and rosy and round...
But where in the World can a Helper be found ?"

"It can't be young Rudolph - his nose is too bright.
It can't be a Gnome, since he'll hammer all night.
It can't be a Snowman - he's likely to melt.
The Penguins can't fly - and they won't fit my belt."

"A terrible problem," agreed Santa's Wife,
(Who secretly jumped at the chance of her life).
She pulled on his jacket, his boots and spare beard,
And looked so impressive - Old Santa Claus cheered.

"Just watch out for aircraft and comets and such,
And hot-air balloons. And don't swerve too much."
But all Santa's warnings were lost in mid-air -
Since brave Mother Christmas was no longer there !

****

Next morning, the Reindeer (with antlers all bent)
Touched down with the sleigh - no one mentioned the dent -
While Deputy Santa wiped soot from her brow
And, dropping the reins - made a big, modest bow.
SO...

If your new Space-Games smell fragrant and sweet;
Or your stocking's been ironed, or your room looks too neat;
Or someone has hoovered the house overnight;
Or the sink in the kichen is sparkly white...

Or you hear a soft laugh in the wide, morning sky -
Just yell: "You're a Star !"
As you wave her good bye.

****

SANTA'S SHRINKING SUIT.

****

Mother Christmas couldn't stop
Herself from rudely giggling,
As Santa squeezed inside his suit
With heaves and huffs and wriggling.
The buttons flew - He wheezed and blew -
His chins were gently jiggling !

"What's happened to my Christmas Kit ?"
Said Santa, turning white.
"My scarlet jacket's far too small,
My belt is far too tight...
My zips won't zip - I dread my trip
Around the sky tonight."

"Your outfit hasn't changed one bit,"
His jolly Wife explained:
"It hasn't shrunk. It's YOU that's grown !
I know you've stretched and strained,
But midnight treats - And tempting sweets
And puddings should be blamed."

"In fact," she added cheerfully,
"Your problem's NO surprise -
So don't feel stressed or sorrowful,
Before you ride the skies.
The children know - You're kind and so,
They love your shape and size.

Then Mrs. Claus nipped out to find
Where COMFY clothes were kept -
She brought a bigger, better suit...
And now, Old Santa leapt
Inside the sleigh - And ZIPPED away
To YOUR house, while you slept !

But Mrs. Santa smiled and said,
"This happens EVERY year !
He'll race and zoom from room to room,
As magic gifts appear...
And soon begin - To look SO thin
And super-fit -
He'll CHEER !"

****

A MERRY MUDDLE.
****

Old Santa chose new glasses - the posh, expensive sort...
Which sadly weren't as magical
Or manly as he thought !

For one thing - they were wonky;
For another - they were blurred,
So when the Christmas postbag came
He couldn't read a word !

He squinted through the lenses,
He tried his very best,
But in the gloom of winter, well...
He panicked. Then he guessed.

That's why, on Christmas Morning
Our Gran got a Giraffe !
(Although she says she clearly asked
For slippers and a scarf).

The Boys just gazed in horror
At a heap of frilly frocks;
The Girls (who'd asked for scooters)
Found a Rocket in a box.

Our Mum was rather puzzled
With a Kit to Build-a-Boat;
And Dad, who'd hoped for gadgets,
Found a small but greedy goat.

Perhaps YOU'VE had disasters too,
Perhaps YOUR heart has sunk -
When, groping through your stocking,
You've discovered piles of junk ?

Perhaps Old Santa should be told - by phone, or text, or letter:
DON'T buy glasses from the Gnomes -
Your OLD ONES work much better.

****

SANTA'S SEASONAL TONGUE - TWISTER.

****

(Read it slowly - then see how FAST you can go,
without tangling your tonsils.)

Santa Claus is stomping in the starlight,
He's stuffing stuff in stockings
On a stormy Christmas night...
But he's sooty and he's sneezy,
While the sleet and snow grow breezy,
So he's huffing and he's puffing,
While his sleigh
Sways
Out of sight !

****

SNOW STORM
****

Oh
I am a merry old Santa -
I've lived here for years with my sack...
I've never been flying.
Or frozen. Or trying
To whirl round the World and whizz back !

Oh
I am a homely old Santa -
I'm jolly and shiny and fat.
My dome (small yet classy)
Has skies blue and glassy...
And snow-storms that swirl round my hat.

Oh
I am a patient old Santa -
I've never been heard to complain...
But sometimes my roof shakes
With TERRIBLE earthquakes !
Take cover -
They've started again !

****

DRONING ON.
****

This winter, Old Santa swapped Rudolph
For a gadget that flies on its own:
Not a milk-float or lorry
Or Super-Store trolley -
But a High-Speed Delivery Drone.

Which means that you won't hear (at midnight)
A jingle or clattering hoof -
Since the point of a Drone
Is - it drops like a stone
And demolishes most of your roof.

So DON'T ask for anything fragile,
Or presents that weigh half a ton -
If they land on your head
And they flatten your bed,
Your Christmas won't feature much fun.

Of course, we could all write to Santa
And ask him to dig out his sleigh -
It's creaky and tragic...
But powered by MAGIC
And that's what we love.
SWOOP AWAY.

****

(Or if you're a real Pilot, you'll shout: "CHOCKS - AWAY !")

178

SANTA'S CHRISTMAS.

****

Whenever you see Father Christmas
He'll be laughing his loud: "Ho ! Ho ! Ho !"
For however unhappy he's feeling inside,
He must never let anyone know.

But one year, alone in his work-shop,
He sat on his bench, feeling sad
As he stared at a huge pile of parcels
For each child, for each Mum and each Dad.

He knew that he should have felt happy -
The Reindeer were raring to go...
The sky was beginning to darken
And the sleigh stood outside in the snow.

"It doesn't seem fair," he said glumly,
"When I work really hard all the year,
Then fly round the skies every Christmas
To sprinkle a sackful of cheer !"

With a sigh, he pulled on his red jacket,
His belt and his big fluffy hood,
Then went off to visit the children
And the grown ups who'd tried to be good.

By morning, the journey was over,
He was weary and covered in soot.
He had crawled down a million tight chimneys,
And round every tree - gifts were put !

He saw the North Pole in the distance,
And he knew he would soon be back home -
But without any stockings or baubles,
He was dreading his Christmas - alone !

179

He tied up the Reindeer and fed them,
Then kicked off his boots in the hall -
"I'm fed up with Christmas," he muttered,
"And I don't think it's jolly at all."

BUT...

All of a sudden, he chuckled !
For the workshop was flooded with light -
The Gnomes and the spare team of Reindeer
Had planned a surprise half the night...

There were toys for Old Santa to play with,
And slippers to warm his cold feet;
There were hand-knitted scarves from the Snowmen -
While his Wife cooked his favourite treat.

(Now, keep going and you will find Santa's Happy Ending.)

The Polar Bears brought him some ice cream;
Plus sweets when the games had begun.
There were crackers and cakes and some carols,
And a tree with a star - just for fun.

SO

These days, whenever you see him,
Wherever you happen to go -
You'll know that he isn't pretending
When you hear Santa's LOUD:

"HO ! HO ! HO !"

****

(I think Santa's favourite treat is Christmas Pudding !)

TWO JOLLY SANTA SONGS.

****

1.

To The Tune Of: 'Humpty Dumpty".

****

Father Christmas jumps in his sleigh,
Brings our presents
For Christmas Day.
Toys in our stockings
And toys on our tree...
AND
One special toy he has made just for
ME !

****

****

2.

To The Tune Of: 'Jingle Bells'.

****

Santa Claus, Santa Claus,
He wears scarlet suits
And jolly scarlet trousers that
He tucks inside his boots -
Oh !
Santa Claus, Santa Claus,
When he sleeps at night,
He wears scarlet jim-jams
BUT
His fluffy beard is
WHITE !

****

SLEIGH SOLUTION.
****

Without a flying Reindeer
There's just ONE way I know
To find Old Santa's Grotto in the land of ice and snow.

You can't rely on Penguins, since you'd have to swim the sea !
You can't ride on a Polar Bear -
He'd eat you for his tea.

You can't ask Mister Snowman
Since he has no legs - or feet !
And the Fairy's far too busy - though her tiny smiles are sweet.

SO...

You'll have to find a Genie in a bottle. Or a lamp -
He'll grant your dearest wishes
When you save him from the cramp !

He'll whisk you on his Flying Rug to Winter World at last -
And there you'll meet the Christmas Team
And all the jolly cast.

You'll see the Magic Workshop
Where Gnomes build trains and cars;
Jack Frost will wave his silver wand, to paint the trees with stars.

You'll help the Elves fill Santa's sack ! You'll climb aboard the
sleigh -
As Father Christmas rings his bell
And chuckles: 'Chocks Away !'

You'll watch the comets swirl and swoop,
You'll clap and shout: "HOORAY !"
Then (in a flash) you'll find yourself - in BED ! On Christmas
Day.

And as you seize your stocking - at your window you will see
Your Genie zooming through the sky
And waving
Gratefully !

****

A CAUTIONARY TALE.
****

A ghastly child called Gordon Greedy
Wanted toys he didn't need - He
Asked for gadgets, gizmos, games,
Expensive ones with flashy names...
His Christmas List went on for ever,
But did he whisper: "Please ?"
NO - NEVER !

On top of that, he loved to munch -
All day long he'd chew and crunch.
His parents tried to change his ways,
But still he piled his plates and trays
With sweets and crisps and cakes with cream,
Until his Granny had to
SCREAM !

And even though young Gordon wrote
To Santa a DEMANDING note...
The dear old Saint just shook his head -
Threw tons of gifts on Gordon's bed,
And tried to guess the schoolboy's weight...
Then joined his Reindeer Team to
WAIT !

When dawn peeped through the window pane,
Young Gordon (ready to complain)
Saw all the things he's asked for ! WOW !
The mounds of gifts heaped anyhow.
While high above the horrid child
Old Santa raced away and
SMILED...

Now, creaks and groans shook shelves and door
In Gordon's room - then creaked some more...
And, like an earthquake, bed and boy
Fell through the floorboards ! Oh - what joy
To see the silly child admit
He'd over done it. Just a
BIT.

"I've learned my lesson," Gordon moans.
"Next year, there won't be broken bones,
Or demolition. Or a crash.
I'll simply ask for loads of
CASH !"

****

YOU KNOW WHO.
****

(For Book-Worms !)

Mrs. Claus cried: "Santa !
It's almost midnight. Look!"
But Father Christmas had his nose - Inside a HUGE, fat book.
"I thought I ought to read it,"
(His voice was rather gruff)
"Since every blooming child this year - Wants Harry Potter
stuff..."

"There's Harry Potter costumes;
And Harry Potter hats;
And blooming Harry Potter wands - And owls and toads and rats;
And Harry Potter card-games;
And Lego Sets, of course,
And Harry Potter blooming brooms." His voice was growing
hoarse.

"That blooming Harry Potter,
He's gone and pinched MY tricks !
Admittedly, I like to steer - A sleigh instead of sticks...
But I invented Quidditch
(As everybody knows)
The Reindeer play with Snowballs - And the Snitch is Rudolph's
nose."

"I'm the one who walks through walls
When chimneys can't be found.
I'm the one who grants your wish - Then leaves without a sound.
I'm the one who rides the sky
(A rare activity)
And I'm the one who's famous for - Invisibility."

So - don't forget, this Christmas
When the night is dark and bleak,
When you hear a distant jingle - Or the floorboards gently
squeak;

And you see the shiny footprint
Of a large and frosty shoe -
It COULD be someone spooky...
But it could be
YOU KNOW WHO !

****

SANTA'S FROZEN BLUES.
****

"I'm feeling rather grumpy - Now that Christmas Eve draws near
-
In fact, I'm almost bored to tears
With children's lists this year...

It seems to me that half the kids - Want blooming Frozen stuff !
Like Frozen Films and Castle Kits...
They just can't get enough
Of Frozen Toys and Frozen Frocks - And Frozen Sticker Books,
And blooming Frozen Olaf
With his funny Frozen looks !

The Elves say they have gone cross-eyed - With all the Pale-
Blue-Twinkles,
And as for Me and Mrs. Claus -
We've both grown Pale-Blue-Wrinkles.
I know the blooming film includes - A Princess brave and
strong...
And jolly ! Which is good, EXCEPT
That blooming 'Frozen' Song -

It jangles round the Grotto - Like an ear-worm in my brain.
I've tried to turn it off, but AAAARRRGH !
It's soon switched ON again !
And on and on and on and on - I'm trying to ignore it,
But all the little Snow-Girls
And the Fairy still ADORE it.

I must admit the endless Blues - Have made a change from PINK
-
But what's become of Festive Red ?
My spirits start to sink.
Has EVERYONE forgotten - All the facts they used to know ?
Like: I'm the one whose friends are made
From magic and from snow...
And I'm the one with Reindeer - As the Elves would all agree,

189

So - if ANYONE is frozen,
Well...
On Christmas Night - It's ME !

But never mind. It's twelve o'clock - And time to LET IT GO !
And if those Blues make children smile,
I'll still say: "Ho, Ho, Ho !"

****

And now we're flying to the far end of the Earth !

EMIGRATION EQUATION.
****

If Christmas could come in the Summer -
Would it be half as much fun ?
Would we swap stockings for beach-bags ?
Then hang them outside in the Sun.

If lunch could be served at the seaside
Where would our Christmas Tree stand ?
Would we eat barbecued pudding,
And sandwiches made from real sand ?

If Grandad could doze in a deckchair -
Would he want slippers from me ?
Perhaps he'd prefer flappy flippers
And go for a dip in the sea ?

If Granny could bask on a sun-bed,
Would she want warm woolly clothes ?
I think she'd prefer a Bikini -
And spend the day painting her toes ?

If Mum had a say in the matter
What sort of gift would she choose ?
Would she decide on a wet-suit
And water-skis rather than shoes ?

If Dad sighed for sledges and snowballs,
Would he build Sandmen instead ?
Would he play games with a Starfish ?
And let his nose glow 'Rudolph Red' ?

If Santa arrived on a Surf-Board
Pulled by a Kangaroo Team -
Would he wear shorts and a sun-hat ?
And would he deliver ice-cream ?

If Christmas could come in the Summer
Would it be half-way as good ?
Would we enjoy all those picnics ?
Would we ?
I'm sure that we would.

****

In Australia, Santa's Sleigh still jingles -
but it IS pulled by a Kangaroo Team !

(And now - we're travelling back in time...)

THE DINOSAURS' CHRISTMAS.
****
(For Eli, Tommy and Dylan.)

The Dinosaurs didn't have Christmas -
A rather sad fact to remember.
No presents. No puddings. No crackers.
No candles. No cakes. No December !

Those poor little Dinosaur children,
They didn't have stockings at all -
So what could they do in the Winter
When snowflakes were starting to fall ?

I just hope I'm WRONG - and at midnight,
A jingle was heard in the dark !
And high in the sky, something glittered...
A comet ? A magical spark ?

While a Dino-child watched, full of wonder
As a shadow swooped down from afar -
The Creature wore bells and a saddle,
Its nose seemed to shine like a star !

Its massive great wings gently folded,
Old Santasaur slid from its back,
He carried a Dino-Sized parcel,
And football-shaped rocks in his sack !

Then happiness rang round the mountains,
As Dinosaur families played
Favourite games - 'Hunt-The-Boulder'
And 'SNAP !' till their dinner was made.

So maybe - that's how the fun started,
With starlight and blizzards that blew !
While Santasaur waited for ages
For Snowmen and Sleighs to come true...

193

And that's why our children love Winter -
And love those old Dinosaurs too.

****

THE MILLION POUND QUESTION.
****

Old Santa sat and sweated
In the cruel yet comfy chair -
And wondered - did he REALLY want to be a Millionaire ?
If he failed the final question
There would be no Happy End -
He was left with just one Option...He would have to phone a
Friend.

But the Snowmen couldn't help him
Since their brains were made of ice;
And the Workshop Gnomes were busy, so they couldn't give
advice.
While the Penguins just fell over,
And the Bears were tucked in bed -
So he scratched his head and whiskers- and he rang a Child
instead.

"Excuse me. This is Santa.
Last year, I'm fairly sure,
I left a new computer propped against your bedroom door.
I only hope you've used it,
I only hope you know...
Who IS the Saint of Children ?" The Child said: "Half a Mo..."

There came a frantic tapping,
Then a voice that shouted: "COOL !
This lap-top that you gave me - says you've been a silly fool."
The Question-Master giggled,
"You must tell me very soon -
It's nearly time for adverts - and a Christmassy Cartoon."

So Santa, looking modest,
In a voice quite shy and hoarse,
Said: "Who's the Saint of Children ? Well - the answer's ME of
course !"

Then everybody stood and cheered,
The Reindeer yelled: "HOORAY !"

And Santa spent his winnings
On a Super-Sonic Sleigh !

****

(It's TRUE. Saint Nicholas is the Saint of Children -
and he's also called: Santa-Claus.)

MY DAD.
****

My Dad believes he's Santa Claus.
A secret hard to hide !
He's always so excitable
Each year, at Christmas-Tide.

He dangles decorations round
The pictures and the ceilings -
And though we think he wastes his time,
We NEVER hurt his feelings.
He hangs a hundred red balloons,
Which perish one-by-one -
And though we think he wastes his breath
We NEVER spoil his fun.

He races home with angel-chimes
And fairies for the tree,
And though we think he wastes his cash.
We NEVER let him see.
He props some carrots by the tree
For teams of passing Deer,
And though we laugh behind his back
We NEVER let him hear.

He hangs our stockings by our beds,
The tiptoes out again,
And though we children need our sleep
We never ONCE complain.
At twelve o'clock he's dressed in red,
He's padded, pleased and proud,
And though we hear him clump about
We NEVER laugh out loud.

He claps his hands as dawn arrives,
He spots each toy and present -
And though we'd rather snooze and snore
We've NEVER been unpleasant.

197

He opens games and magic tricks,
Plus toys that whirr and clatter -
And though our Dad is slightly daft...
Today, it doesn't matter !
SO
If you have a Dad like ours
Who THINKS he's Santa Claus...
Remember - if you make HIS day,
He'll probably make YOURS.

****

Santa - Kit !

Beard →

Toys and Sweets

← Hat

A WHEELY GOOD CHRISTMAS.

****

(Written for Sir Ken Dodd.)

One far and foggy Christmas time,
When sheets were cold and noses sore -
I told Old Santa all about
The present I was longing for.

I chewed my crayons, drew my dream,
I wrote my hopes and wishes down;
Then watched my message whirl around
The sooty chimneys of the town.

On Christmas Eve, my stocking hung
As sad and empty as despair...
I'd been a fool, I'd asked too much.
My gift would NEVER fit in there !

I'd asked for something much too big.
Too wonderful. Too bright and red.
Old Santa Claus would have to leave
A little bag of sweets instead.

****

I must have slept, because I thought
I heard a bell, a squeal of brakes,
A rumble and a nasty thump,
The sort of groan an Old Man makes...

I told myself: "Your stupid mind
Is playing childish tricks on you -
THERE'S NO SUCH THING AS SANTA CLAUS,
And Christmas Wishes don't come true."

I closed my eyes. The night whizzed by,
I woke and wriggled out of bed.
My stocking still stood empty

BUT
Against my wardrobe - BRIGHT and RED

My perfect present leaned and gleamed !
Brand new (apart from one small dent).
The very bike I'd hoped to see...
The gift that Santa Claus HAD sent.

The Moral (if you're wanting one)
Is: Trust your dreams - and then
HAVE FUN.

****

THE CHRISTMAS SECRET.
****

One year, I made a wish so secret,
So precious,
I would not write it down,
Or call it from my window,
Or whisper it to the Moon.
Instead, I spoke it inside my mind
Over and over
As Christmas came closer.

My friends teased and prodded.
My family leaned down
With questions that smelled of puddings and pies.
The High Street Father Christmas
Searched for clues in my eyes,
But my wish could not be found
In any shop or shiny catalogue.

"The REAL SANTA will know,"
I told myself
While other children roared their demands
And stamped their fierce feet
Like small Emperors.

On Christmas morning
All the bright presents
Bulged in my stocking or loomed beside my bed...
But I slipped past them to stand
Breathless with hope
On the frosty doorstep.

And there were the boot-prints
Marching across the silver grass.
There was the tangle of red thread
Caught in the holly bush;
There was the faint jingle of bells
On the winter air.

201

And there,
In the cold fingers of our apple tree
Was my secret gift.

In a moment, it melted and fluttered away
As softly as a white owl's feather -
And I turned back to the indoor world
Of toast and warm surprises.

But the magic has stayed with me
To this far, grown up day.
And now it is time to loosen its ribbon of stars
And share it with YOU.

****

CHRISTMAS AND THE NEW YEAR

THE BOXING DAY BLUES.
****

Everyone bored,
New toys ignored,
Who can afford
Boxing Day ?

Batteries gone flat,
Torn paper hat,
Feel cross and fat -
Boxing Day.

Crackers all gone,
Presents look wrong,
Too small, too long,
Boxing Day.

Tree starts to sag,
Time seems to drag,
Moan, fight and nag...
Boxing Day.

Gifts piled in mounds,
Jangling sounds,
Head throbs and pounds,
Boxing Day !

Cold feet, cold plate,
Kitchen a state,
Who doesn't hate
Boxing Day ?

Games thrown on floor,
Wreath falls off door,
No patience - no more
Boxing Day.

Ban it I say,
Take it away,
It's over ! Hooray !
Boxing Day.

****

MADE BY HAND.
****

My Granny had knitted a jumper -
It took her a month, if not more.
It was baggy in all the wrong places
And the sleeves stretched right down to the floor.

The colour was well worth avoiding,
And the front didn't quite match the back -
The neck was so tight, it was painful
And the whole effect looked like a sack.

She wrapped it with love and with tissue,
Then propped it in front of the tree...
And I knew (without reading the label)
She intended that jumper for ME.

I opened it up very slowly
And struggled for something to say -
I knew, if I injured her feelings,
I would ruin our whole Christmas Day.

Her eyes watched my face as I fumbled,
And of course, I had no choice at all.
"Oh Gran," I said. "Thanks. This is perfect -
My old one was scruffy and small."

I wore the creation to please her
And waited for insults galore...
But instead of the jokes I was dreading,
I came home with orders for MORE !

So now, my old Gran makes a fortune
By turning her wool into gold,
And though we all LOOK pretty funny -
Not one of us EVER feels cold.

****

THANK YOU LETTERS.
****

As soon as the Big Day is over
There's something that HAS to be done...
A task that we all view with terror,
And no one could ever call fun !

I'm given a pen and some paper,
A check-list and stamps (second class),
Then I sit, staring out of the window -
At scraps of mince-pies on the grass.

I'd rather be drying the dishes,
Or washing the dog with a sponge;
Than trapped here, indoors with a note-pad
Too troubled to tackle the plunge.

I'd rather be tidying cupboards,
Or changing the sheets on my bed;
I'd even scrape fluff off the lamp-shades -
But here I sit, scratching my head.

There's that pretty pink rug from an Aunty
(Though the colour I'd chosen was black),
There's the book that says: 'Love from your Granny',
So I can't take the boring thing back.

There's the gadget that came from an Uncle -
(I still can't decide what it's for);
There's the Calendar, so cute and soppy,
I've stuck it on poor Grandad's door .

There's a dog made by one of our Cousins -
It squints in the creepiest way !
There are soaps, there are socks, there are smellies -
My courage is starting to fray...
No wonder I'm biting my biro -
And I can't think of ONE thing to say !

So I'll just have to hide in a corner,
Or sing: 'La-la-la' in my head...
And as for those letters - no thank you !
I'll write them tomorrow instead.

IT'S THE THOUGHT THAT COUNTS.
****

(GIRL:)

I really don't mind what I'm given -
After all
It's the thought that's the thing...
But I'd really be thrilled with a scooter,
Or a kitten who pounces on string.

I'd love to be given a token -
Or trainers to whizz down our street;
Or maybe a book full of stories;
Or a chocolate Santa to eat.
I wouldn't mind pictures to colour;
Or a torch for some dark, spooky nights;
I'd even be grateful for pencils...
Well, wouldn't you know it ?
It's

TIGHTS.
****

(BOY:)

I really don't mind what I'm given -
After all,
It's the thought that's the thing.
But I'd really be thrilled with a skateboard,
Or a robot to circle and ping.

I'd love a new game for my laptop -
Or some Lego to tackle with pride;
Or maybe a big bag of toffees ?
Or a tent I could sleep in - outside !
I wouldn't mind mountains of joke-books;
Or a puzzle that's packed in a box;
I'd even be grateful for pencils...

209

Well, wouldn't you know it ?
It's

SOCKS.
****

(Now, both together - but try to smile !)

Thanks very much for the presents
Thanks very much indeed -
We really don't know how you do it...
They're exactly what we need.

****

(Now - it's Winter. Time for frost, snow and dark, dark nights.)

FLIGHT OF FANCY.

****

Today, there's magic in the air -
The oak tree shakes his tangled hair
To spill his golden treasures where...

The frost has painted pathways white.
And in the ivy, diamond bright,
The spider webs are strung with light.

And all the morning, wonders grew -
The sky became a field of blue,
Where birds, like Summer flowers flew.

The willow tree bent low to greet
The grasses dancing at her feet,
And Winter sang a song so sweet...

 I saw, between the holly leaves,
How every scarlet berry weaves
A spell my hopeful heart believes.

And now, the fiery sun sinks down
To gild the rooftops of the town,
While Evening whirls her starry gown...

Today was magical. And rare.
And I should know -
For I was there.

****

(I wrote this poem for a lovely, funny man called Sir Ken Dodd.)

211

Now - a little bit of magic just for YOU.

A NEW YEAR WISH.
****

What can I wish you -
When New Year arrives ?

A sunrise of Happiness,
Warming your lives.

A casket of Laughter
To share with a friend.

A packet of Patience,
Till gloomy days end.

A huge heap of Hope
For our planet, our home.

A pathway of Joy,
Where your dreams brightly roam.

And

A parcel so precious
So strong and so kind -
It will comfort your heart,
It will comfort your mind...

Or keep you as warm
As the wings of a dove,
The best wish of all -
Lots of Love.

Lots of Love.

****

But of course - some of us are wishing for SNOW...

SNOWFLAKES.
****

There are snowflakes made from paper
On each window and each wall;
There are snowflakes in the kitchen,
And the bathroom and the hall.

There are snowflakes in our bedrooms;
On each cupboard and each door;
There are snowflakes (slightly trampled),
On the carpets and the floor.

There are snowflakes hung from ribbons
To annoy us on the stairs;
There are snowflakes painted silver
On our dishes and our chairs.

There are snowflakes on the ceiling;
There are snowflakes on the tree;
There are snowflakes, large or little,
In every place I see...

There are snowflakes in a blizzard
Every place those flakes can go !
There are FAR too many snowflakes
BUT
There isn't any
SNOW !
****

(Oh dear ! That is much too sad. Let's try the next page...)

At last, in 2021 - Mother Nature gave us all a wonderful treat.
I'm sure you've guessed - it was a fall of real SNOW.

****

SNOW TIME !!
****

Roll up, now ! Roll up ! This is Nature's Big Show !
Look out of your window,
With eyes all aglow...
There are feathery flakes,
Softly drifting - let's go !
Race down your staircase to welcome the SNOW.

Pull on your boots and your bright, woolly hat;
Wrap yourself warm
As a squirrel or cat;
Run with the others
While snowballs go SPLAT !
Then build a great boulder - a Snowman wants that !

Pat him with shovels and give him a smile,
Add twiggy fingers
Plus buttons with style !
A carrot for sniffing...
And in a short while
A holly-leaf crown - from a shivery pile.

Now you see sledges that slither and swoop,
They skid down the slopes
With a crash - or a whoop !
Some children scream,
Some circle and loop -
And three little dogs want to slide with the group.

But soon you grow hungry - it's time for your lunch,
The crowds start to leave,
With a sigh and a scrunch.
You race your way home,
For a sandwich to munch...

But the snow is still waiting !
Hooray !
Let us
CRUNCH !

****

The BEST Snow-Creatures we saw this year were - a Snow-Wolf and a Snowy-Saurus (which looked just like a Stegosaurus) !

THE SNOW-WOLF.

****

Our neighbour's made a Snow-Wolf -
Which gazes at the Moon,
The Stars, the Sun, the Rainbows,
Plus a bouncy, blue Balloon.

Her mouth is wide and waiting
For the other Wolves to HOWL...
But she's only seen a Robin
And a silent, spooky Owl !

I think that's why she's left us
To trace her Snowy Pack -
And I hope, next year, she'll find us
When we YOWL:
"Snow-Wolf - Come back !"

****

THE SNOWY-SAURUS.

****

(For Eli and Ben.)

I've built a Snowy-Saurus -
With a bit of help from Dad.
The wind is sharp and icy
But
My Snowy-Saur is glad...

He doesn't like the Sunshine -
His Snow-Friends dripped and plinked,
They lost their nice, new buttons,
And were GONE before he blinked !
So...
I hope he'll live for ever
And will never be
EXTINCT.

****

217

AFTER THE SNOW.
****

(I borrowed this friendly idea from a lady-vicar on the radio.)

This morning, as I trudged the path
Where muddy trickles ran,
I spied a heap of lumps and bumps
That used to be a man !

I found his frosty carrot;
The hat he'd worn with style;
His twiggy hands - and best of all
His happy Snowman Smile.

****

Other girls have many things
Too dear for me to buy.
Other girls are talented -
But I am small. And shy.

Yet - other girls are sad because
The snow is just a pile
Of slush and ice and bits of sticks
Where sculptures stood a while...

But in my secret pocket
Still
I keep a Snowman's Smile.

****

THE TWELFTH DAY OF CHRISTMAS.

****

(This is when the decorations usually come down.)

Throw away the mistletoe,
The tinsel and the holly -
It's too late now for paper-chains,
It's too late to be jolly.

Sweep away each silver star,
Each needle and each berry -
It's too late now for fairy-lights,
It's too late to be merry.

Clear away the Christmas cards -
Come on. Make it snappy !
It's too late now for party hats,
It's too late to be happy.

For Christmas is over,
There's no more good cheer -
So we can be GLOOMY !
(At least - till next year !

****

(But don't be too sad - Spring is on its joyful way.And before it arrives -
there are candles, and stars, and 'Candle-Light Tales'.)

219

WINTER NIGHTS.
****

The night comes too soon,
And the Winter is cold -
But the Darkness - we hide her
With curtains of gold.

We light our rooms
With dancing flames,
We fill the sky
With fiery names,
Rockets painting
Spiral traces,
Torches high
And shining faces,
Sparks as bright
As dragon scales,
Smoke in coils
For fireside tales,
Windows glinting
Row on row,
Shiny trees
To gleam and glow,
Until the shadows
Loom and
GROW...

Winter is cold
And the night comes too soon -
But Darkness - she gives us
The stars
And the Moon.

****
(Now for a Candle-Light Tale for a Winter's night)

(The next poem came to me in a silly dream...and it is full of noisy
Sound Effects. So have fun!)

THE FRIDGE ON THE STAIR.
****

There's a fridge at the top of the steep castle stair
Though last night I'm certain
A fridge wasn't there !

It simply appeared without warning, today -
It's monstrous and old
And it's blocking my way.

And from its insides I am sure I can hear
The squeal of a rat,
Or a whimper of fear.

Or maybe the hoot of a mythical owl,
Or else an unearthly
And ominous howl.

The brute starts to tilt, then it stumbles downstairs
On flat, rusty feet,
Two clattering pairs...

Now its door lurches open. It gapes like a cave !
Is that any way
For a fridge to behave ?

It's lumbering closer. Its cold breath accosts me.
And an icy voice crackles:

"CAN SOMEONE DEFROST ME ?"

****

(Can you make the sounds of: a rat; a whimper; an owl; a howl;
clattering feet; a creaky door, and an icy voice ? Good luck.)

****

(This is Clare's favourite, spooky tale -
but it's for older children and grown ups.)

THE STRANGER.
****

The hour was late when the Stranger
came to the moor's bleak edge.
The short cut - was dangerous but
he was lured from the guiding hedge.

All for the gift he carried
and the message he must bear.
He paid heed - to his greater need,
Though his conscience might cry: "Beware !"

The wind grew icy and savage
gnawing his flesh like teeth.
Black as pitch - gaped a waiting ditch
As it snatched a prey for the heath.

Out of the murderous darkness
in a weaving mesh of fog,
Lifting jowls - with curdling howls
Rose the massive form of a dog...

It flung itself at the Stranger -
and its coat was thick and warm.
So it lay - 'til streaks of day
Brought a rescuer with the dawn.

****

The Stranger leaned on the pillows
and spoke from his drowsy bed -
"Was he yours - that dog on the moors ?
But for him, I was surely dead."

"Ah, no," said the man. "My Pilot,
he died ten years ago.
Tired and old - and stiffened with cold
From saving a man
In the snow."

****

Hooray. A ghost story with a warm ending.
But now it's time to say good night.
I wish you all happy dreams and a wonderful New Year.

****

ABOUT THE AUTHOR.
****

Clare Bevan used to be a teacher and she still loves visiting schools.
Her first book won the Kathleen Fiddler Award, which was very exciting!
Now, she likes writing poems for children, and her verses can be found in more than one hundred anthologies.
Clare lives with her husband in a cobwebby house and her favourite hobbies are:
Performing her poems; wearing hats; feeding the birds in her garden, and riding a big purple tricycle AND she loves Christmas of course!